The Dante Inferno:

Nicolò's Wedding Deception

*The Dante Dynasty Series:
Book #3*

by

Day Leclaire

USA Today Bestselling Author

Please Note

This is a work of fiction. Names, characters, places, and incidents either are the product of the author's imagination or are used fictitiously, and any resemblance to actual persons, living or dead, business establishments, events or locales is entirely coincidental.

Cover Design by Melyssa Naujoks, 2019

For more information, please visit my website:
http://www.DayLeclaire.com

Book Description

A liar and a thief ... or his Inferno mate?

When Kiley O'Dell claims to own half the mines that contain Dantes legendary fire diamonds, the family sends the most ruthless and cynical of the brothers, Nicolò Dante, the family troubleshooter, to negotiate with her. Neither expect the legendary Inferno to strike, sending both up in flames.

Nicolò suspects Kiley's claim is a con. And he'll do whatever necessary to get to the truth, even chase a panicked and fleeing Kiley. To his horror, she darts into traffic and is hit by a cab before he can save her. After she wakes, she insists she has amnesia. Now he's certain she's conning him, and he has a way to prove it.

Turning the tables on Kiley, Nicolò claims she's his wife. What he doesn't expect is for The Inferno to tumble them into a fierce love affair. Which is the real Kiley? The sweet, passionate woman in his bed, someone he'd do anything to keep, or the crafty con artist he first met? And what will happen when she discovers they're not married at all, that far from being her loving husband, Nicolò is out for vengeance?

Lover or liar? Devious or delectable? Only The Inferno can determine which.

Dedication

To Donna Totton, for being the best sister-in-law in the world . . . and for your constant support and assistance.

Thank you!

Table of Contents

Other Titles by Day Leclaire

The Dante Inferno:

The Dante Dynasty Series

Some blazes, once ignited, can't be extinguished. Just one burning touch connects a Dante with his soul mate.
The Inferno ... curse or blessing?

Sev's Blackmailed Bride, Book #1

Marco's Stolen Wife, Book #2

Nicolò's Wedding Deception, Book #3

Lazz's Contract Marriage, Book #4

Luc's Unwilling Wife, Book #5

Rafe's Temporary Fiancée, Book #6

Draco's Marriage Pact, Book #7

Gianna's Honor-Bound Husband, Book #8

Becoming Dante: Gabe, Book #9

Dante's Dilemma: Romero, Book #10

Forever Dante: Lucia, Book #11

Prologue

Nicolò Dante anticipated trouble the same way he anticipated marriage—one part dread, and two parts determination to find a way out of the whole unfortunate mess.

Some men found a certain inevitability to the sorry state of "wedded amiss." His two brothers, Sev and Marco, had eventually succumbed to the entire process like the not-quite-proverbial rams to the slaughter. Well, not him. He had enough trouble in his life without looking for more.

And right now, that trouble took the form of Kiley O'Dell.

"We need you to look into this," his eldest brother, Sev, instructed. "According to the documents Caitlyn uncovered, there's a distinct possibility that this woman may own a substantial interest in Dantes' fire diamond mine."

Such a simple statement, yet the implications were dire, and could cause endless problems for Dantes' jewelry empire, an empire whose fame was built on the lure of fire diamonds. They could be found nowhere else in the world, except deep within the bowels of a Dante mine, and they were coveted by everyone from royalty to heads of state to the local shopkeeper around the corner.

Nicolò's expression darkened. "Our dear sister-in-law should have kept her nose out of those old papers. They've brought us nothing but grief." He lifted an eyebrow in question. "Does Marco have no control over Caitlyn?"

Sev shook his head in disgust. "You really don't have a clue, do you?"

"I'm probably the only one who does." Nicolò leaned a hip against his older brother's desk. "What's the point of being so damn charming, if he can't use some of it on his own wife? He tricked her into marriage, didn't he? Now that he's got her, the least he can do is keep her out of trouble."

Sev crossed his arms across his chest, his burnished gold eyes brilliant with laughter. "Keep digging that hole, bro. Your Inferno bride will be delighted to bury you in it when you eventually come across her."

"Forget it." Nicolò made a brisk slicing movement with his hand. "As far as I'm concerned the family curse—"

"Blessing," Sev corrected mildly.

"Blessing? Hell, it's more like an infection."

Sev tilted his head to one side and considered the description. "That's an interesting analogy, although I'd say The Inferno is closer to a melding."

Nicolò allowed a hint of curiosity to show. "What was it like when you first felt The Inferno for Francesca?"

"Are you finally admitting it exists?"

"I'm willing to admit you and Marco believe it does," Nicolò conceded grudgingly.

"And Primo."

Nicolò dismissed that with a swift shake of his head. "Our grandfather is the one who has perpetuated the legend all these years. It offers a convenient excuse to explain lust, no more and no less."

"Now you sound like Lazz," Sev said. "But if that were true, Caitlyn never would have been able to distinguish between Marco and Lazz, considering how difficult it is to tell the two apart. And yet, she picked out her husband without any doubt or hesitation. And she did it under the most extreme circumstances. Wasn't that enough to convince you?"

Nicolò couldn't deny fact. Nor could he rationalize what he'd seen that day. But that didn't mean he'd allow Sev to draw him into a discussion about the veracity of The Inferno. "You still haven't explained what it's like."

An odd smile drifted across Sev's mouth and his eyes seemed lit from within, filled with an unsettling combination of pleasure and satisfaction. "When I first saw Francesca, I felt a physical pull, as though we were somehow connected by a thin tenuous wire. The closer we moved in proximity, the stronger the connection between us. It kept growing until it became so powerful, I couldn't resist it."

"That's it? You felt physically attracted?"

"Shut up, Nicolò." There wasn't any heat behind the demand, just amused impatience. "Do you want to know, or don't you?"

"I asked, didn't I?" Though why he bothered, he couldn't say. Horrified fascination, perhaps. Or perhaps forewarned was forearmed. The instant he felt anything similar, he'd get the hell out. Get out long before he did something as outrageous as Sev—like blackmail his future wife into first leaving their competitor and working for Dantes, and later still agreeing to a pretend engagement. Clearly The Inferno did strange things to the men and women it mated. "Something happens when you touch, doesn't it?"

"A shock."

At the reminder, Sev kneaded the palm of his right hand with the fingers of his left. It was a habitual gesture, one Nicolò had seen both his grandfather Primo and his brother Marco imitate. They all claimed it occurred as a result of The Inferno, a lingering residual from that first touch. Even Caitlyn rubbed her palm periodically.

"A shock like static electricity?" Nicolò prompted.

"Yes. No." Sev grimaced. "It's a shock, yes. But it doesn't really hurt. It surprises. Then it seems to meld us. Complete the connection. After that, it's done. There's no going back. You've been matched with your soul mate and you're permanently joined for the rest of your lives."

Damn. Nicolò didn't like the sound of that. He preferred having his options open, to have a variety of choices. In his position as Dantes' troubleshooter, he required the freedom to jump from one creative opportunity to another should the need arise. Experiencing such a total loss of control didn't appeal to him at all. The Inferno stole that control, forcing its will on unwilling subjects. And though he didn't mind bending on occasion, so long as it happened to be in the general direction he was headed anyway, he resented like hell the concept of being broken, stripped of power, and forced along a path not of his choosing.

"Well, with luck The Inferno will be clever enough to leave me alone," Nicolò said lightly. "Now tell me what you've discovered about Kiley O'Dell."

"Nothing."

Nicolò's brows tugged together. "What do you mean nothing?"

"I mean that since the question of who actually owns the fire diamond mine broke in *The Snitch*—"

"Damn interfering gossip rag."

Momentary amusement flashed across Sev's face. "Now you sound like Marco. Not that it matters. Apparently, the O'Dell woman reads *The Snitch*." His amusement faded. "She's come forward demanding a meeting to discuss the situation. A meeting you're going to set up. Unfortunately, we haven't been able to get any substantive background info on her. At least, not yet."

Nicolò stared, appalled. "You expect me to go in blind?"

"I don't see what choice we have." Sev waved that aside as though an unimportant consideration. That's what he got for making his job seem so easy. "Listen, just hear her out. Primo bought that mine fair and square. Find out why she thinks her family might still have a legitimate claim after all these years. Then stall while we put some P.s on this." A fierceness settled over Sev's face. "I don't have to tell you how much we stand to lose if Kiley O'Dell's claims prove genuine."

"Dantes will go under." Nicolò didn't phrase it as a question.

Sev nodded. "Everything we've worked to rebuild over the past decade will have been for nothing. We need to find out what proof the O'Dell woman has that she's a legitimate owner in the mine and then keep her happily oblivious while we find a way to take her down."

Nicolò's expression hardened. "Then that's what I'll do."

"Nic—"

"I understand how important this is." It was probably the most delicate job he'd ever handled, as well as the most difficult. "I'll find a way to keep her off balance."

"Tread lightly." At Nicolò's questioning look, Sev elaborated. "Her claim could be genuine. We don't want to do anything to set her against us. We want an amicable resolution, not a pitched battle."

Nicolò shook his head. "Then she shouldn't have started this war. Because one way or another I intend to finish it."

Chapter One

Kiley O'Dell wasn't at all what Nicolò expected.

But then, neither did he expect the tidal wave of desire that slammed through him, rendering him deaf and blind to everything but the woman standing in the doorway of her suite at Le Premier. He saw her mouth move, but the sound refused to penetrate the roaring that filled his ears, a roaring that demanded he take this woman and make her his. To put his mark on her in every way possible. To possess her and bind her to him until neither of them could escape.

No. He dropped his head and fought the sensation, fought for all he was worth. He flat-out refused to accept this feeling, flinching from the very real possibility that it might signify the start of The Inferno.

No. Way. In. *Hell.*

This woman spelled trouble from the top of her dainty red head to the tips of her tiny red-coated toenails. And he refused to allow trouble into his life, his bed, or his heart. No matter what it took, he'd put an end to this sensation. It couldn't possibly be that difficult. It only required a single, simple solution. All he had to do was figure out what that solution was and The Inferno would pass him by.

Lifting his head, he took a second to study Kiley O'Dell, using every scrap of creative skill at his disposal to search for a way out of his latest predicament. But nothing came to him and he simply stood and stared at her.

Her name suited her. She stood no taller than a minute, with a taut, lithe figure that packed just enough curves in just the right places to tempt a man to explore every inch of that creamy white skin. She wore her hair long and it fell in heavy strawberry-blond curls to the middle of her back. She also possessed the most stunning pair of pale green eyes he'd ever seen, eyes that dominated her triangular-shaped face.

"Mr. Dante?" she asked, clearly repeating herself. Her cultured voice contained a low, musical quality that fell easily on the ears. "Is there something wrong?"

"Nicolò."

He shoved the single word from between clenched teeth. Did she have any idea how hard he struggled to act with a modicum of propriety while instinct clawed at him, urging him to snatch her up in his arms and carry her off to the nearest bedroom?

Possibly, since a hint of wariness crept into her regard and a pulse kicked to life in the hollow of her throat, betraying her instinctive response to him. A response not all that unlike his own, if he didn't miss his guess. A streak of color highlighted her arching cheekbones and he could almost smell the whiff of desire that perfumed the air between them. Oh, yeah, this wasn't good.

She recovered far swifter than he. "I'm Kiley O'Dell. Thank you for taking the time to see me."

Everything about her appeared quick and decisive, from the sharp once-over she gave him to the way her gaze leapt from him, to the hallway, and then over her shoulder to the spacious hotel room. He couldn't help but wonder if that last glance was a final check to make sure she'd properly set the scene for their encounter.

"Come on in," she said, stepping to one side.

She didn't bother offering her hand, which suited him just fine. Considering the overwhelming hunger her appearance aroused it would be downright foolhardy to touch this woman. Not with The Inferno currently on the rampage, cutting a swathe of destruction through the Dante males.

Not that he believed in The Inferno. Hell, no. He hadn't when Primo first told the tale. Nor when Sev and Marco tried to convince him they'd both experienced it the first time they'd touched their future wives. And he damn sure didn't intend to start believing in The Inferno now. Not even with this desperate need filling every empty space inside him with a want so huge he could barely contain it all.

"Would you like something to drink?" Kiley tossed the question over her shoulder while she crossed the plush carpet. She moved with a hip-swinging stride that drew his gaze to her pert, rounded backside lovingly outlined by a pair of trim black slacks. He caught back a groan. Was it deliberate, or another aspect of the stage she'd set for their meeting? "I have sodas," she continued. "Or something stronger if you feel the need."

Whiskey. He'd kill for a double shot of single-malt. "I'm fine, thanks."

"Do you want to talk first or get straight down to business?"

"What's there to talk about?"

That had her turning around. A crooked smile tilted her mouth, giving her an almost gamine appearance. "We could take a stab at making this a friendly get-together. You know, exchange the usual pleasantries people do when they first meet."

Okay, he'd play along. "Like?"

"Like . . . Tell me what you do at Dantes, Nicolò."

"I solve problems."

Laughter gleamed in those odd green eyes, turning them spring-leaf bright. "And I'm your current problem?"

"I don't know." He lifted an eyebrow. "Are you?"

She shrugged. "Time will tell."

She folded her arms across her chest and leaned her hip against the back of a richly upholstered divan. She took her time, studying him at her leisure. Searching for a weakness? he couldn't help but wonder. If so, she'd have a long, fruitless time of it. The moment stretched, thin and sharp as razor wire. She broke first.

"It's your turn," she prompted gently.

"My turn . . . what?"

"To ask a question." She released a tiny sigh. "That's how this works, you see. When you're getting to know someone, you exchange pleasant chitchat in order to ease the tension."

"Are you tense?"

"You're kidding, right? You don't feel it?" She punctuated her questions with her hands, their movement through the air as brisk as everything else about her, yet graceful for all that. "Hell, Dante, it's thick enough to scoop out of the air and dish up for dessert."

So she felt it, too. It wasn't just his imagination. "Is that what you suggest? That we move straight to dessert?"

"Is that your way of resolving our problems?" she countered. Heat and awareness broke from her in splashy waves, building on his own. "Do you really think you can seduce my share of the mine out from under me? Is that your creative solution to this particular problem?"

Yes. "No."

"Good. I'm relieved to hear it."

"Because you don't own a share in the mine." He took a step closer, just to gauge her reaction. She didn't move, but he caught the slight tautening of the muscles across her shoulders and the brief widening of her eyes before she relaxed. *Gotcha.* She was good at this little game she played, but he was better. "Since you don't own any part of the mine, getting you into bed won't make any difference to the eventual disposition of your claim."

To his surprise, she laughed, the sound light and unfettered. "I'm so glad we have that out of the way."

"Funny. It still feels like it's right here between us."

It was her turn to take a step closer, to push at the electrical current sizzling between them like a live wire. "Shall we get it out of the way, Dante?" she dared. "It would be easy enough."

She reached for the first button of her blouse and thumbed it through the hole. Then a second. And a third. The deep V of her neckline revealed an intricate heart-shaped locket on a thin silver chain. Then he caught a flash of vibrant red, a sharp note of color trapped between the milky whiteness of her skin and the unrelenting blackness of her blouse. Before he could stop himself his attention dropped from her breasts to her low-riding slacks. Did she wear a matching bra and panties set? Did she conceal hellfire and brimstone beneath the pitch-black of her clothes?

He slowly looked up, his gaze clashing with hers. How long would it take him to find out? Judging by the hungry expression on her face, not long at all. Her fingers hovered above the final two buttons.

"Finish it."

His voice sounded as though it had been put through a shredder. He deliberately took the final step that separated them. Only the merest breath of space held them apart, that space awash with turmoil. Desire roiled there, along with mistrust and suspicion. It was a desire he intended to destroy, while nurturing the mistrust and suspicion.

"Finish it," he repeated. "And show me your true colors."

She jerked back. Where before her movements flowed, now they stuttered. Color stained her face and turned her eyes evergreen dark with horrified disbelief. She fumbled in her effort to rebutton her blouse, jamming the wrong buttons into the wrong holes.

"What the hell was I thinking?" she muttered. The question seemed aimed at herself rather than at him. She shook her head as though to clear it before demanding, "What are you doing to me, Dante?"

"You're the one doing the striptease, lady. Don't blame me if I expect you to put up or shut up. Now do you have proof to back up your claim that you own part of Dantes' mine, or is that what you were in the process of showing me?"

He'd rattled her, something he suspected didn't often happen with the self-possessed Ms. O'Dell. "You feel it, too," she insisted quietly. "Don't try and tell me I'm imagining things."

"And yet, I'm not the one taking off my clothes."

To his surprise, amusement rippled past the heat and turmoil and gentled the flames. "Too true, Dante. I'll have to watch my step with you. It would appear you bring out the wanton in me, though who knew there was any wanton in there to begin with." She shook her head in disgust. "Live and learn."

Taking a deep breath, she circumvented the divan she'd been leaning against earlier and gestured toward the coffee table in front of it, one littered with papers. She waved him toward a second divan, situated opposite the first.

"So, let's get down to business. You want proof. Here's my proof." She picked up her first batch of papers and shoved them across the table toward him. "My grandfather was Cameron O'Dell. He and his brother, Seamus, were the original owners of the fire diamond mine that your grandfather, Primo Dante, eventually purchased. I've just given you copies of my grandfather's birth certificate, his death certificate and a deed showing that he was a legitimate half-owner of the mine."

Nicolò leafed through the papers. "My understanding is he died before the sale to Primo was finalized."

"True. But that would have merely transferred his share of ownership to any surviving children—my father, to be specific." Kiley tossed another document in his direction. "Here's a copy of Grandfather's will confirming that fact."

"Do you have your father's birth certificate proving he was born before Cameron died?"

Another piece of paper came sailing across the table. "Right here." She rested her elbows on her knees and leaned forward. Her locket swung out from beneath her misbuttoned blouse. It was a curious piece of jewelry, thick and chunky, consisting of fragments of silver that had been laced together to form the heart. "Your grandfather may have paid off Seamus, but my great-uncle didn't have the right to sell my father's share of the fire diamond mine, despite what he may have claimed at the time."

Nicolò took his time studying the documentation, though he suspected he'd find everything in perfect order. A con artist would have made certain of that. What he hoped to uncover while he pretended to read was the slip in logic. It didn't take lng to key in on it.

"Why has your family waited so long to bring this matter to our attention?" he finally asked. "Why didn't you file a lawsuit decades ago in order to get your fair share?"

"I didn't know I might be an owner. As for my father . . ." A hint of some painful memory came and went in her eyes. "I can't ask him that question since he died when I was little more than a baby."

Nicolò allowed a hint of sympathy to show. "You were raised by your mother?"

"What difference does that make?" she asked in sharp retort.

He lifted an eyebrow. For some reason what he intended as a throwaway question had provoked an unguarded response, and clearly a defensive one, which made it all the more interesting. It told him a lot. Without even intending to, he'd hit a hot button with her. It showed him how tight a control she kept over her words and emotional responses. Until now.

"You were the one who suggested we get to know each other better. That's what I'm doing." He pushed a little harder. "Tell me about her. What's her name? How did she make ends meet after your father died?"

Kiley's mouth tightened. "I think you're stalling."

He shrugged. "Believe what you want. I'm just trying to figure out whether she's in on this little scam or if you came up with it all by yourself."

"It's no scam."

"So you say. But I suspect Seamus will tell a far different story."

Her movements slowed, fluttering to stillness like a bird settling to its nest. It was a "tell," an unconscious look or movement—or lack thereof—that betrayed a lie. He'd always had an innate ability to pick up on them, a prime reason his brothers refused to play poker with him. He could always tell when they were bluffing, just as he could with Kiley.

She moistened her lips with the tip of her tongue, a second, more obvious "tell." "Seamus?" she repeated.

Nicolò took a stab in the dark. "According to Primo, he's still alive." He offered an expansive smile. "Tell you what. Why don't you sit tight for the next few days and enjoy the amenities Le Premier has to offer, while I track him down? I'm sure he can clear up this confusion in no time."

"Give me my papers." The words escaped, raw and harsh.

Without a word he gathered them and passed them across the width of the coffee table to her. Their fingertips touched during the exchange, just the merest glancing brush of skin against skin. A brief flash of electricity burst between them, sizzling for an instant, but not quite catching. Nicolò shot to his feet.

"What the *hell* are you trying to pull?" he demanded.

She shrank back against the divan, her eyes huge and vivid in a pale face. "I don't know what you're talking about."

For the first time in his entire life, Nicolò ignored instinct and went with pure suspicion.

"Sure you do. You read *The Snitch,* didn't you, Ms. O'Dell? You read about the diamond mine, no question there, since it's what prompted you to contact us. But you also read all about the Dantes and their little Inferno problem. And it gave you the most brilliant idea. Let's gather up these old family papers, you tell yourself, and see if you can't fake a case for partial ownership in the fire diamond mine. And if that doesn't work, let's see if you can fake The Inferno."

She shot to her feet. "You are hands-down certifiable."

"Then how do you explain that little pop of electricity?"

"How the hell should I know? Maybe your brain short-circuited." She hugged the documents to her chest. Giving him a wide berth, she skirted the coffee table and crossed to the door of her suite. "I think you should leave."

Nicolò followed her to the door. "I'm not going anywhere. Not until we have this out. Because, we're not done here. We're not even close to done."

"Yes, we are. First thing in the morning I intend to contact my lawyer. Until then, get the hell out of my room."

He leaned in close, so close he could feel the tiny charges of electricity skipping off her and latching onto him. Pulling and tugging him toward that ultimate commitment, attempting to sear him with that final fateful touch. "This isn't over, you know."

Her breathing grew jagged and he could see his want reflected in her eyes, a mate to his own, just as he could sense their heartbeats thundering as one. He almost sealed her mouth with his, the temptation nearly overwhelming. It took every ounce of self-control to pull back at the last second. Without another word, he opened the door and stepped into the hallway. The door slammed closed behind him.

Nicolò stood there for a moment. He could still feel her, right through the damn door. She was leaning against it, fighting the same attraction he fought, telling herself, just as he did, that what she felt was insane. Impossible. And to be avoided at all costs. He shook his head in disgust. Right there with you, Gorgeous.

Nicolò headed for the bank of elevators and took a car to the main floor. Once there, he hesitated. The lobby offered a spacious sitting area, with groups of chairs arranged in cozy settings. Large, carefully tended ferns, bushes, and even a few ornamental trees created oases of privacy.

He eyed a set of chairs that were discreetly screened, while still offering a prime view of the elevators. Instinct kicked in again, growing too loud to ignore. In his thirty years of existence, he'd learned not to question that gut-deep demand. It always signaled something his subconscious had picked up on that his conscious mind hadn't caught up with quite yet.

Giving in, he took a seat and waited. It didn't take long.

No more than five minutes later Kiley came barreling out of one of the elevators with that brisk, hip-swinging stride he now realized was her natural way of walking. She wore her hair up and had thrown on a black jacket to match her slacks. Very businesslike. She made a beeline for the concierge, her foot tapping impatiently as she waited for him to answer her question.

Nicolò sensed a purpose behind her actions. She had a destination in mind and he intended to find out where . . . and with whom. It would be interesting to see if she had a partner in crime. The concierge must have given Kiley the answer she needed, for she rewarded him with a broad smile that seemed to cause the man's brain to short-circuit the same way Nicolò's had earlier. Then she spun around and started toward the lobby doors. And that's when disaster struck.

Even though there was absolutely no reason for her to notice him or glance his way, even though he was practically buried in a jungle of shrubbery, the instant she came level with his position, she stiffened and her step faltered.

Whatever connection had been forged in those few minutes they'd spent together crackled to life, sending out tendrils of awareness.

Time slowed and stretched. The chatter of voices and clatter of humanity grew muffled and distant. Even the light seemed to dim, leaving just the two of them within its brilliant embrace. With unerring accuracy, Kiley's head swiveled in his direction and her gaze locked with Nicolò's. The instant she spotted him, her eyes widened in shock. Acute distress followed on the heels of her shock.

Her distress caused an unexpected stab of concern that threw him off stride. He didn't want to feel anything for this woman. Unfortunately, he couldn't deny fact. During their brief time together, something had sparked to life, and it was more powerful than anything he'd ever experienced before.

Time resumed its normal pace and Kiley shot toward the entryway and whisked through the glass doors embossed with Le Premier's name and logo. Nicolò followed, instinct urging him to run, the hunter giving chase to his prey. He hit the sidewalk outside the hotel just as she reached the corner intersection. People were still crossing, though the crossing light blinked a bright red hand of warning. She threw a quick glance over her shoulder. Spotting him, she darted into the crosswalk just as the light changed.

He saw it coming before it happened. A cab broke around a slow car, accelerating directly toward the intersection. Clearly, the driver didn't realize Kiley was there. Nicolò thought he shouted a warning. He knew he broke into a run. The driver didn't spot her until the very last instant. He hit the brakes at the same instant she tried to leap out of the way, but it was too late. The cab's bumper clipped her with just enough force to send her somersaulting into the air before connecting with the pavement. Even as Nicolò pelted toward her, he reached for his phone. He hit the emergency link without even looking and barked the information at the operator the moment the call went through.

He reached her side and knelt down. She didn't move. Didn't even seem to breathe. From what he'd seen of her fall, she'd been sent flying toward the opposite sidewalk and hit her head on the curb. Vibrant blush-red hair flowed around her, still shimmering with life, while her pallor warned of something far different. Her locket rested against her cheek like a kiss.

"Kiley!" He didn't dare touch her, though he wanted to. And then he saw it, the slow, steady rise and fall of her chest, and he almost lost it.

"I didn't see her." The driver of the cab appeared, staring down at Kiley and wringing his hands. Unabashed tears rolled down his bearded face. "She came out of nowhere."

"I saw what happened. It wasn't your fault." Nicolò's mouth tightened. The blame was all his, not the cab driver's.

"Is she—" The cabbie broke off, swallowing hard. "Is she . . . ?"

"No. I've called for an ambulance."

As though in response, sirens wailed in the distance. A small crowd gathered around them and Nicolò kept them back with a single terse command, followed by a look so black that it sent most of the onlookers scurrying on their way.

The police arrived minutes later, the ambulance shortly after that. Nicolò watched helplessly as they secured the area and tended to Kiley. He vaguely remembered giving his identification. Vaguely recalled claiming Kiley as his own, because on some visceral level he knew that she was. Her well-being had now become his responsibility.

All through the hideous ordeal, he watched the EMTs stabilize her, watched them attach endless medical equipment to her, watched them fit her head and neck with protective devices. And the only thing he could think about was that if he hadn't followed her, she'd never have run. She'd never have been hit by the cab. Never would have been injured.

He'd been so caught up in proving her a con artist, he'd put her life in danger. Based on the grim glances he saw the emergency personnel exchange, he may very well have killed her. He closed his eyes, forcing himself to face facts.

There was a connection between them whether he wanted it or not. That spark of electricity they'd experienced earlier hadn't been part of her con. She'd been as surprised by their physical reaction to one another as he had. The truth was this woman could be his Inferno mate. Since they'd never fully touched, he couldn't be one hundred percent positive. But he doubted they needed complete contact. Deep inside he sensed the truth, sensed it with every fiber of his being.

The Inferno had sent him his soul mate. Granted, she wasn't the one he'd have selected for himself. But by driving her to act so impetuously, he could very well have destroyed their future "might have been" before he ever got to know her. He'd claimed he didn't want an Inferno bride.

It looked like fate had given him exactly what he wanted.

Chapter Two

"Have you lost your mind?"

Nicolò glanced over his shoulder toward the hospital waiting room to make certain they couldn't be overheard. Spying a few curious looks, he addressed his brother Lazzaro in Italian. "No, I haven't lost my mind. It's my fault she's in here. If I hadn't been running after her, she would never have—"

Lazz waved that aside with a sweep of his hand. "You told me that already," he replied in the same language. "So now, in addition to having a claim on our fire diamond mines, Kiley O'Dell can sue you for chasing her in front of a cab. Is that what you're telling me?"

"Yes. No." *Damn it.* Why did Sev have to send the logical Dante? "You don't understand."

"Then explain it so I will. And while you're at it, explain to me why they're calling you Mr. O'Dell."

Nicolò folded his arms across his chest. "I need regular updates about Kiley's condition. And since they only discuss a patient's condition if you're a relative, the hospital staff may be operating under the misunderstanding that I'm her husband."

"They what?" Lazz shoved a hand through his hair while he fought a perceptible battle for control. "Don't tell me this is another one of your creative solutions."

"You never complained when my 'creative solutions' worked to Dantes' advantage."

"Damn it, Nicolò!"

"Look, it just happened, okay? They needed information about her and since I had her purse with her identification and medical cards, they leapt to a conclusion I didn't bother correcting, especially since it works to our advantage."

"It works to our advantage right up until someone recognizes you. It isn't like the Dantes are exactly low profile here in San Francisco. Our faces have been plastered all over the gossip magazines in recent months, or have you forgotten that minor detail?"

"Sev, you, and Marco, may have been prominently featured in *The Snitch,* but I've been maintaining a low profile. As for Kiley, I plan to play the part of Mr. O'Dell for the time being. Eventually, I'll straighten everything out. Until then—" Nicolò handed his brother Kiley's purse "—get her information and give it to our head of security. Tell Juice that I need anything and everything he can discover about her as quickly as possible."

"I'm already ahead of you. I put him on it yesterday."

Nicolò nodded. "Perfect. Also, send someone over to Le Premier. Considering the amount of business we throw their way I don't think the hotel will give you too hard a time about packing up her belongings and checking her out. I want regular updates on this, Lazz. And once Juice's done gathering any surface info on her, I want him to dig for more. Tell him to dig deep. I want to know everything from what size clothes and shoes she wears right down to what brand of makeup she uses. Everything," he stressed. "Got it?"

"Why? What are you planning?"

Nicolò didn't dare answer that one. "It's still fluid."

Lazz shot a hand through his hair. "Aw, hell."

"Look, when I have all the details figured out, I'll let you know. Also, stop by my place and feed and walk Brutus, will you? I don't know how long I'm going to be hung up here."

"You've pulled some wild stunts in your time, but this . . ." Lazz shook his head. "This one makes all the others seem almost normal."

"This stunt won't last long. As soon as she wakes, the jig'll be up and I'll have to finagle some new plan."

"Like a way to get us out from under a massive lawsuit?"

Nicolò's expression fell into grim lines. "That's only a possibility if she ends up blaming me for the accident as much as I blame myself."

"You better hope like hell she doesn't."

The sudden appearance of a nurse saved Nicolò from having to reply. "Excuse me, Mr. O'Dell?"

"How's Kiley?" Nicolò immediately asked, turning his back on his brother.

Compassion darkened the nurse's eyes. "All I can say for certain is that she's stable. The doctor would like to see you and I'm sure he'll fill you in on the particulars." She inclined her head toward a nearby hallway. "If you'll follow me?"

He instantly fell in step with the nurse, only realizing afterward that from the moment she showed up he'd completely forgotten his brother even existed. Turning a corner, the nurse opened the door to a small conference room barely larger than a cubicle. A doctor sat at a table, making notes in a tight, rapid scribble.

Flipping the chart closed, the man rose and offered Nicolò his hand. "I'm Dr. Ruiz."

"Just give it to me straight. She's alive, right?" Nicolò demanded tightly.

"Alive and stable," Ruiz confirmed. "But she took quite a hit. It was miraculous, given the circumstances, that she didn't break anything. She has various lacerations that we've stitched up and a deep hematoma to her left hip. It's going to be quite painful and make it difficult for her to get around comfortably for a while."

"And the bad news?"

"As you're aware, she experienced a head trauma. A concussion. There's been some minor swelling to her brain, but she's responding to the medications we're giving her to reduce it and all the scans are clear."

"Is she awake?"

The doctor shook his head. "She woke briefly and seemed highly agitated and disoriented. Since then she's been unconscious."

One of the skills that made Nicolò so good at his job was an innate ability to read people. "What aren't you telling me?" he asked.

Ruiz's mouth compressed. "I'm sorry, Mr. O'Dell. Head traumas can be tricky. Until she wakes, we won't know the full extent of her injury. She may be perfectly fine, with perhaps a slight loss of memory from around the time of her accident. Or it could be far more extensive. You should prepare yourself for the worst, and hope for the best."

"When can I see her?"

"She's in intensive care. You can peek in for a minute or two right now. Then I suggest you go home and get some rest. We'll call if there's any change."

Ten minutes later, an ICU nurse escorted him into one of the dozen three-sided rooms that comprised the unit. Kiley appeared small and frail in the bed, with various wires and tubes connected to her, while a dirge of machines beeped softly in the background. He wished she would open her eyes so he could see the vivid color brimming with that unsettling combination of hot awareness and keen intelligence, so he'd know she'd fully recover from her injuries.

He felt the kick that urged him to go to her, to link their hands and complete the bond he felt between them. But he couldn't. Wouldn't. As though sensing a similar awareness despite the drugs sedating her, she stirred restlessly. Clearly, The Inferno—if that's what it was— called to her, as well, for she muttered in whatever twilight land she occupied. Within moments a nurse appeared in response.

"She senses you," she said, before offering a sympathetic smile. "You'll need to go now. If you'll leave a phone number we'll call with any updates."

He did as instructed, but found he couldn't wait for them to contact him, and returned to the hospital first thing the next morning. The ICU nurses all turned to watch him with broad grins that gave him a second's warning before he stepped into Kiley's room and heard her attending doctor say, "Here's your husband now."

Both Nicolò and Kiley froze, staring for an endless moment at each other. Then she shook her head in wild-eyed disbelief. "That's not possible," she denied in no uncertain terms. "There's no way he's my husband."

Nicolò bit back a curse. "Dr. Ruiz—"

"Don't panic, Mr. O'Dell." The doctor tossed a reassuring glance over his shoulder. "We warned you she might have memory issues."

"No. I'd remember if I'd married him," Kiley argued.

"It's all right, Mrs. O'Dell," the doctor said in a soothing voice. "Your loss of memory is a result of your accident."

Nicolò shut his eyes. Time to 'fess up. "She's not—"

The doctor spoke at the same time, his voice rumbling over top of Nicolò's confession. "Kiley, you don't even remember your own name," he said gently. "It's perfectly natural you wouldn't remember you have a husband. I suggest we take this slow and easy. Your memory could come back at any point. Hours. Days. Possibly weeks. In the meantime, we can move you out of ICU and into a regular room while we run a few more tests."

"Why won't you listen to me?" Kiley's gaze landed on Nicolò before flinching away. Tears filled her eyes and her voice rose with each word, growing steadily more shrill and hysterical. "I'm telling you this isn't my husband. He can't be. I'd know if he were."

Ruiz signaled to one of the nurses, who began to prepare an injection. "Mr. O'Dell, I'm afraid I'm going to have to ask you to leave. Once she's had time to calm down and get accustomed to what's happened, you can come back."

Nicolò inclined his head. "Of course. If you'd just give me a second."

He acted without thought, running on sheer instinct, responding to a call no one heard but him. Crossing to Kiley's side, he reached down to take her hand in his. Behind him, Ruiz voiced an objection, while Kiley hissed in dismay as she drew back in a vain attempt to avoid his touch. He ignored everything but the demand screaming through him, one that insisted he finally act on the urge that had been clawing at him since the moment he'd met this woman.

He forcibly took Kiley's hand in his.

The Inferno struck with more ferocity than Nicolò believed possible. Even the machines trilled in momentary alarm before subsiding again into a steady rhythm. Never before had he experienced such a powerful connection. It felt as though every emotion he possessed flowed from his hand into hers before slamming him with a backwash that left him drowning in desire.

He responded without thought. Without giving her time to protest, he bent down and took her mouth in a kiss of utter possession, hard against soft, determination overwhelming uncertainty. She tasted even sweeter than he'd imagined, soft and warm and—after a momentary hesitation—receptive. No. More than receptive. Eager.

He couldn't resist. He swept inward, taking advantage of her unstinting welcome. Never had he felt such a reaction when he'd kissed a woman, as though every aspect of the touch and taste of her had branded him. A certainty filled him, a certainty that no other woman would ever be quite right for him, except this one. The softest of moans, hungry and eager, slipped from her mouth to his, welcoming him home.

And in that moment, he could no longer escape the simple truth.

This woman belonged to him.

Kiley froze at the first touch of her husband's hand, overcome by a sensation so all-consuming, it rendered her speechless. Fiery heat shot from palm to palm, almost painful in its intensity, before settling into a warm, steady connection that soaked deep into that point of melding. Second by second, with each beat of her heart, desire pierced straight through flesh and sinew and bone, until it invaded every part of her. It seemed to lap through her veins, filling her to overflowing with a heavy, irresistible want.

And then he kissed her.

It was a first kiss, worthy of fairy-tale legends. It was also impossible to compare to any that might have come before, since fate had veiled any such occurrences. Even so, she found it the most incredible experience in her very short memory. His mouth ate at hers, his hunger unmistakable, threatening to consume her with that single, unbelievably delectable kiss. Every instinct she possessed screamed to life, telling her this was her man. That he belonged to her and no one else. Her response came without thought or reason. She opened to him, unfurling like a flower beneath the blazing heat of the sun.

He possessed her mouth and she gave back to him with unstinting generosity. In that instant she didn't care who she was, or who this man claimed to be. All that mattered was that this moment never end. Where before all felt alien and unfamiliar, this she recognized. This she knew. Slowly, he pulled back, his breath escaping in a heated rush, his eyes burning with black fire. She could read in his expression all that she felt, a mating of tumultuous emotions.

She sensed on an instinctive level that she and this man had become permanently entangled, heart, body and soul. But how was that possible? How could something as basic as joining hands, or exchanging a single kiss, cause such an undeniable reaction? How could this simple contact bind her to a complete stranger with such relentless power?

Her reaction to his touch told her she knew this man, regardless of what she'd claimed only moments before. Slowly she lifted her gaze to her husband's. Or at least, the man who claimed her for his wife.

Her opinion of him hadn't changed in the few moments since he'd first stepped into her room. He remained fiercely handsome, a god of war, with hair and eyes of the deepest ink and a stare that silenced with a stony glare. He wore his hair longer than convention dictated and it fell to his neck in heavy waves. Maybe they would have tightened into actual curls if he hadn't subdued them, no doubt with a single forbidding look, the kind he currently had trained on the nurses and doctors surrounding them.

"Who are you?" she demanded. She waved away his response before it could even form. "I know you claim you're my husband. I mean, what's your name?"

"Nicolò. You call me Nicolò." A smile warmed the stark coldness of his features, touching a mouth that had left an indelible stamp on her own. "Except when you're angry with me. Then you choose a few more colorful terms of endearment."

"And how often does that happen?"

His smile grew, stunning in its beauty. "Often enough. We both have rather tempestuous personalities."

His gaze lifted to the medical personnel gathered around her bedside and he jerked his head toward the curtain that screened the cubicle. Without a word they filed from the room. It didn't come as any surprise they acquiesced. She had a strong suspicion few dared to argue with Nicolò, and those few who tried, didn't hold out against him for long.

"I'd also like to set one fact straight," he said the moment they were alone. "My name isn't O'Dell, it's Dante. Nicolò Dante. When you were first brought in, everything happened in such a confusing rush I didn't bother to correct the error."

He watched her closely as he gave her this latest piece of information, his penetrating look making it almost impossible to think rationally. "I don't understand," she replied. "If we're married, why do we have different last names?"

He shrugged. "We haven't been married long. And you haven't decided whether or not you want to take on all the baggage associated with mine."

She had questions, so many they spun, jumbled, around in the dark fog of her mind. She seized one at random. "You said we haven't been married long. How long is 'not long'?"

"Only a few days. It was a whirlwind affair."

For some reason that upset her, possibly because she'd hoped for more. Proof of a lengthy, established history that he could document in word and picture. A connection stretching back across the empty recesses of her mind. Something that would anchor her in this confusing world in which she'd awoken. Instead, he could only offer a mere snippet to sum up the whole of her life.

"A whirlwind affair," she repeated. Her eyes narrowed in thought. "Somehow, Nicolò Dante, you don't strike me as the impulsive sort. I'd have pegged you as a very deliberate sort of guy. Someone who gets what he wants when he wants it, no matter who or what stands in his way. Am I wrong?"

At the question, a mask dropped over his face, sharpening the harshly beautiful features into diamond-hardness. "That's quite an interesting observation after only a minute or two of contact. Or have you remembered something about me?"

Dear Lord, how could she have been so foolish as to wed a man like this? The strength of his personality threatened to overwhelm her, something she wasn't certain she could prevent even if she weren't injured and in a hospital bed. She must have been out of her mind to marry this man, to believe for even one tiny second that she could cage herself with a hungry panther and emerge unscathed. Maybe—in that other forgotten life—she liked challenges. Or maybe she was simply crazy. Time would tell.

"To answer your question, I don't remember you at all," she confessed. "I wish I did, because then I'd understand how I came to be in this predicament." She plucked at the sheet covering her. "And in response to your other comment, I'm basing my assumptions about you on how you managed to clear the room with a single look."

He studied her in silence before conceding her point. "You're right. I do whatever it takes to accomplish my goals. My family will tell you I'm the most impulsive of all of them, since sometimes that's what it takes to succeed. Split-second decisions. Thinking outside the box. Finding a creative solution to an impossible problem."

"And us?" she couldn't help asking, lifting her gaze to clash with his. "How does our relationship fit into that dynamic?"

A hint of rueful amusement drifted through the darkness. "Even if I weren't the impulsive sort, you can tell by your reaction to my touch, there were other considerations."

She could make a fairly accurate guess about one of those considerations. "You mean we were attracted physically." She didn't bother to phrase her observation as a question. There wasn't any question about her reaction to him. Or his to her, for that matter.

He studied her in silence for a long, uncomfortable moment. "Apparently, it's far more than a simple physical attraction, Kiley. It goes deeper than that. If it didn't, my touch wouldn't affect you this way. When you lost your memory, it should have severed all of the connections between us." He held up their linked hands. "And yet, it hasn't."

She blinked in surprise to discover their hands were still joined. Despite the warning signals screaming through her system, she accepted the contact between them. More, she clung to it. "You think I recognize you on a subconscious level?" she asked slowly. "Is that even possible with amnesia?"

Again that hesitation, as though he used great care in choosing his words. Apprehension gathered like a hard, tight ball in the pit of her stomach, and she couldn't help but wonder what he wasn't telling her. Endless bits and pieces she had no way of guessing at, let alone verifying. Everything about her life, about his, about their past and present, even any plans they may have made for the future—the details were his to select, to shade if he so chose, and she'd be forced to accept them at face value. Only one person held the key to all the information comprising her former life, a man she had no choice but to trust. Heaven help her!

"Dr. Ruiz said your memory might return, given time," Nicolò said.

He hadn't answered her question, she noticed. Hadn't explained how or why she recognized him on an unconscious level. But his comment roused a far greater concern. "What if my memory doesn't return?"

He didn't sugarcoat it. "Then you'll have from this moment forward." That gorgeous smile flashed again, completely altering his appearance. "I suspect you'll start to regain bits and pieces of your past before too long, especially considering your reaction to me."

"Which reaction?" she asked with a hint of dry humor. "The part where I became hysterical, or the part where I melted into a heap of lust?"

Her question caught him off guard and a laugh escaped his control, the low rumbling sound like distant thunder. "A heap of lust?"

Her cheeks warmed, but she continued to meet his gaze. "Well, what would you call it?"

"The Inferno."

He spoke so quietly, she almost didn't catch his response. She tasted his words on her tongue, repeating them softly. "The Inferno. That's the perfect description for what I'm feeling." Then she made the connection. "Dante's Inferno? Clever."

"I can't claim the description as my own."

"A family joke?" she said, hazarding a guess.

Again, stillness settled over him and the gaze he fixed on her, so dark and damning, almost made her flinch. "A memory, Kiley?" he asked gently. "Or just a good guess?"

Understanding hit and she inhaled sharply. "My God, you suspect I'm faking amnesia, don't you?"

His expression never eased. Nor did the manner in which he stared at her. "Why would you do that?"

"I don't know. I'm the one with the memory loss, remember? So, you tell me. Let's start with how I was injured," she requested.

Much to her relief, he didn't weigh his words this time. "You were hit by a cab while crossing the street. I came out of the hotel just in time to see it happen."

Now he did pause, but she suspected it had nothing to do with choosing what to say and how to say it. She could tell how badly the accident had affected him, could glimpse the horror and helplessness he'd experienced in those final few seconds before she'd been hit. She wasn't the only one damaged when she'd been struck by that cab. His life had also been irreparably changed.

It took a moment for him to gather his self-control before continuing. "As I said, what possible reason could you have for faking amnesia? It was a stupid, regrettable accident."

"But there's something more. I can see it in your expression. What aren't you telling me?"

"We had a fight right beforehand." The admission came hard. "You left the hotel in a hurry. If I'd stopped you from leaving, or if I hadn't delayed going after you, I might have prevented the accident from happening."

She couldn't mistake his sincerity and something loosened inside of her. Apparently, even hard, powerful men suffered from vulnerabilities. It would seem she was his. "You blame yourself, don't you? For the accident, I mean."

His fingers tightened around hers. "Yes."

"What good would it have done if you'd been with me?" She offered a reassuring smile. "Chances are we'd both have been hit by that cab."

Again, that bleak expression. "Doubtful. It's far more likely I would have prevented the incident from ever occurring."

The absolute certainty in his voice amused her. "I see I've married an arrogant man."

"That isn't arrogance, but fact."

She laughed, the sound a bit rusty, but it felt good, nonetheless. "I believe you just proved my point," she said.

Kiley couldn't say when she accepted Nicolò as her husband. Not at first touch, despite the undeniable connection between them. She'd still been too traumatized by her loss of memory at that point to accept much of anything. Granted, the unmistakable surge of lust had convinced her she and Nicolò were two parts of a whole, clearly connected to each other physically. But that hadn't been enough to convince her they were husband and wife.

Perhaps she'd begun to accept their marriage because of the way she'd clung to him throughout their conversation. Or the scorching pain she'd glimpsed when her husband had described her accident. Or maybe it had been something as silly as his admitting she hadn't decided whether or not to take the Dante name as her own. Whatever the cause, the result was she accepted one undeniable fact. They belonged together.

"What are you thinking?" he asked quietly.

"I'm trying to remember, but . . ."

"But, what?" he prompted.

"I'm afraid." It amazed her she confided in him after only knowing him for mere minutes. Maybe it had been like that when they'd first met. In fact, she was certain it must have been. She could practically see their affair unfold as though part of some romantic dream, where they met and connected and established an instant rapport, both emotional as well as physical. It would explain so much about her current feelings for him. "I'm afraid of what I'll find when I do remember."

"Or not find?"

His perception unnerved her. "That, too."

"Now it's my turn to ask," Nicolò pressed. "There's something else. What aren't you telling me?"

For some odd reason tears gathered in her eyes. "I'm afraid if I go to sleep again, I'll lose more of myself, if that's even possible." She whispered the confession, almost afraid of speaking it aloud in case it gave form and substance to the nightmare. "That it'll be like that movie. You know the one? Where she wakes up each day having to start over again?"

"You mean *50 First Dates?*"

"Yes, that's it." Kiley stirred restlessly, an intense throbbing in her hip making her catch her breath before she could go on. "Isn't it ridiculous? I can remember that movie but I can't remember when or where I saw it or who I was with." She shot him a hopeful look. "I don't suppose it was you?"

To her disappointment, he shook his head. "I should warn you we don't know each other all that well. Our relationship really is a whirlwind affair."

She offered a crooked smile, attempting to put the merest hint of shine on a bleak situation. "Then it shouldn't take us long to catch up, should it?"

That won her another grin, one that caused her heartbeat to kick up, a fact duly noted by the surrounding monitors. "Not long at all."

A wave of exhaustion hit her and her eyes began to drift closed. "I'm getting so sleepy. It must be that shot the nurse gave me." Her fingers tightened on his. "Will you still be here when I wake again?"

"I'll be right here. I'm not going anywhere."

So adamant. So solid and reassuring. "Will I remember you?" she managed to ask.

"If you forget, I'll remind you. And if that doesn't work . . ." He lifted her hand to his mouth and pressed a kiss in the center of her palm. "This is one thing you'll never forget."

"You're right. I'll never be able to forget that," she whispered. "Thank you, Nicolò. I'm so glad you're my husband."

And then darkness captured her again.

Chapter Three

"Have you lost your mind?"

Nicolò released his breath in a deep sigh. "I believe that's the same question you asked me last time we had this conversation."

"It bears repeating," Lazz proclaimed. He turned to the oldest Dante brother, Sev, for confirmation. "You can't possibly condone what he's doing?"

"Not even a little," Sev assured. He hesitated for a split second before adding, "Although—"

Lazz shut his eyes. "Oh, no. *Hell,* no. Do not in any way, shape, or form encourage him in this madness."

"It'll give us time to figure out what she's up to," Sev offered. "If she does get her memory back, we'll be prepared. Nicolò will have gathered enough information to put a plan in place."

"Is that straight from legal?" Lazz shot back.

Nicolò fought to keep from massaging his palm. Ever since he'd joined hands with Kiley, he'd been driven by the overwhelming urge to rub the spot where her touch had branded him. It had happened to Sev and Marco after they'd been bonded with their Inferno matches. And now it was happening to him, though he didn't dare let on just yet.

"In case it's escaped your collective notice," he announced, "I'm not asking for anyone's advice or opinion. I'm simply informing you of the latest developments."

"Which includes you continuing to pose as her husband," Lazz barked. "Just what the hell do you suppose will happen when she gets her memory back?"

Nicolò lifted a shoulder in a negligent shrug. "I'll deal with it."

Lazz's twin brother, Marco, spoke up for the first time. "I think the more intriguing question is, what do you intend to do with her if she never regains her memory?" He stared at Nicolò, seeing far too much. "How long do you plan to keep up the pretense? And what do you do with her once you're convinced of her guilt?"

"Or innocence," Nicolò inserted without thought.

Marco's gaze sharpened. "You think that's at all possible?"

Nicolò considered the possibility before reluctantly dismissing it. "No. When we met at

Le Premier, I'm positive she was running a con of some sort. With luck, Juice can uncover the truth. In addition to checking into her background, I had him collect her possessions from Le Premier."

"What did he discover?" Sev asked.

"Nothing helpful." Which only made Nicolò's suspicions all the stronger. "We didn't find anything to indicate where she came from immediately preceding our meeting, or whether she has an accomplice. We haven't found an address book, tablet, or so much as a business card. Her cell phone is a disposable. And her driver's license lists an old residence. She moved from that location—Phoenix, to be exact—eighteen months ago and left no forwarding address."

Sev frowned. "That alone should give us pause," he said. "No one maintains that low a profile unless it's for a reason. I assume you told Juice to continue digging?"

"I did. He has instructions to call me with regular updates I can incorporate into what I tell Kiley about our history together. Until then, I intend to keep her close."

Lazz straightened. "I don't like the sound of that. What history? And just how close are you planning to keep her?"

Nicolò spared his brother an impatient look. "Try applying some of that logic you're so fond of. She's supposed to be my wife, remember? When she's released tomorrow, I'm bringing her home with me. I've already transferred her possessions to my house and have created an entire history of how, when, where, and why the two of us hooked up." All three of Nicolò's brothers shot to their feet, arguing at once. He waited until they ran out of steam before speaking again. "She's still recovering from a serious accident. She has no memory and no one to help her—except her husband."

"What if she's faking amnesia?" Lazz asked.

"Or is running part two of her con?" Marco added.

Nicolò's expression hardened. Then he'd see she regretted playing him for a fool for a long time to come. "All the more reason to have her where I can keep an eye on her. She believes I'm her husband. I intend to play the part to the hilt until I have a damn good reason not to. So far, none of you have offered me one. Once Juice has figured out the truth, we'll decide how to proceed from there."

"Do you have any idea the sort of trouble this could cause?" Lazz demanded.

Nicolò released a laugh, the sound ripe with irony. "It's going to cause more trouble than you can possibly imagine. Unfortunately, I don't have a choice."

The Inferno had seen to that.

"This is where you live?"

"We," Nicolò corrected gently. "This is where *we* live."

"Oh, right." Kiley stared up at the elegant turn-of-the-century Victorian. From deep inside the recesses of Nicolò's—*their*—home came a thundering bass woof that succeeded in rattling the stained-glass windowpanes bookending the front door. She swallowed. "What was that?"

"Ah." A brief smile came and went. "That would be a who. Brutus, to be specific."

"Brutus," she repeated faintly. "And what sort of creature is a Brutus?"

"Dog."

"Huh. It sounds more like a cross between a moose and a lion."

"That would be about right." He waited until she swiveled to face him in wide-eyed dismay before relenting. "He's a St. Bernard. Very gentle."

Time would tell. She took a deep breath and faced the front door once again. She slanted her husband a final glance. "I don't suppose you know whether I like dogs?"

"You love dogs," he stated categorically. "And you're crazy about Brutus. Everyone's crazy about Brutus."

"If you say so."

Nicolò slid his key into the lock and opened the door. A series of thuds drummed through the soles of her shoes as Brutus approached at a dead run. He reached the parquet flooring in the foyer and the speed of his forward momentum sent him skidding across the glossy wood. He slid to a stop inches from where she and Nicolò stood.

Kiley remained frozen in place, utterly petrified by the mammoth animal who probably topped her by a solid hundred pounds and appeared capable of swallowing her whole in a single gulp. The top of his head hovered at shoulder height and every inch of his massive body rippled with hard, lean muscle, while his rich, multicolored coat gleamed with health. He was a gorgeous animal, though right now she found it difficult to summon much appreciation for that fact in the face of overwhelming terror.

Nicolò dropped to his knees and performed some sort of ritualistic man/dog bonding game that had her backpedaling as fast as her aching hip would allow until her spine hit the front door. If she could have melted into the wood and out the other side, she would have.

"Nicolò," she whispered.

He glanced over his shoulder and frowned. "What's wrong?"

She fought to speak around a bone-dry throat. "I think the amnesia may have screwed up my dog appeal."

Nicolò came to his feet, creating a solid barrier between her and his dog. "Don't be afraid. I swear, Brutus is the gentlest animal in the world."

"It's just . . ." She swallowed. "He's so big."

"Yeah, he is," Nicolò agreed. He made a hand signal and in response Brutus dropped instantly to the floor in a sphinxlike pose. "So, we'll take this nice and slow. I'm right here beside you, and I won't let anything bad happen."

"Thanks." He held out his hand and Kiley took it without a second thought. She even allowed herself to be drawn toward the dog, who didn't so much as twitch a muscle. "Why isn't he moving?" It was downright unnerving.

"I've trained him not to." Nicolò offered a reassuring smile. "You're not the first person to be intimidated by his size. So I taught him certain behaviors that make him more approachable and less overwhelming."

"You're going to try and get us to be friends now, aren't you?" she asked with a marked lack of enthusiasm.

"Yup." He sent the dog another hand gesture and Brutus dropped his head onto his enormous front paws. Huge melting brown eyes peered up at Kiley. "Kiley, this is Brutus. Close your hand in a fist and just put it in front of his nose so he can smell you. Don't worry, he'll recognize your scent."

It took every ounce of nerve to do as Nicolò instructed and stoop in front of the huge animal. Closing her eyes and praying she wasn't about to lose half her arm, she lowered her fist to within a few feet of Brutus's snout. The dog's nose twitched and he sniffed her hand. His tail thumped in recognition and he squirmed close enough to lick her. It was as though someone had flicked a light switch. The fear didn't completely disappear, but how could she resist the sweetness exuding from Brutus?

She gave in to temptation and scratched behind his ears. After a few short minutes, her sore hip forced her to her feet and she gingerly stood with an assist from Nicolò. "His coat is so soft," she marveled. "Especially around his ears."

"Don't let him fool you. He's a cagey beast."

"Cagey?"

"It's all about food with this one. Be careful when you're eating because he'll find a way to distract you so he can snitch your meal off your plate." Nicolò interlaced his hand with hers. "Come on. Why don't I take you on the grand tour?"

"I'd love to see the place."

With Brutus leading the way, Nicolò escorted her through the lower rooms, featuring a generous-sized kitchen with a small table set in a bow window, a formal dining room off the kitchen, as well as a beautifully decorated living area. Deeper in, he showed her what was clearly his favorite room, a large den with built-in bookcases, a mile-wide plasma TV and a couch with cushions as soft and comfortable as down.

His cell phone rang right before they headed upstairs and, with a word of apology, he took the call. "What have you found out, Juice?" He listened for a long minute. "Any family other than . . . ? Got it. No, that's quite helpful, thanks. Just what I needed." He disconnected the call and offered Kiley one of the smiles that never failed to ignite a flame of intense awareness. "Sorry. Business update I've been waiting for."

"No problem."

Nicolò paused in the doorway of a large bedroom gilded by late afternoon sunlight.

Leaning against the doorjamb, he waited while she circled the room. "This one's yours. I thought you'd be more comfortable having a room to yourself. At least for the time being."

Surprise held Kiley frozen for a split second. "That's very thoughtful of you," she murmured.

She didn't dare tell him it didn't feel comfortable at all. Instead, it made her feel all the more alone. On the other hand, did she really want to spend the night in his bed? Despite her instinctive reaction to him—an all-consuming passion that defied understanding—they'd only known each other for a few days, at least to the best of her current recollection. Her husband was being incredibly sensitive by not forcing them into an intimate relationship until she'd had time to adjust to their marriage. This situation must be every bit as difficult for him as it was for her.

Nicolò crossed to the closet and opened the double doors. "Your clothes are in here, as well as in the dresser."

Curiosity filled Kiley and she joined him, eager to see what sort of clothing she normally wore, hoping it might help her pick up clues to her personality. The wardrobe was stuffed full, with something for every occasion, though most of the items still had tags dangling from them.

"Why is everything brand new?" she asked.

"You're a Dante now. You needed clothing to match."

She examined the outfits a second time and inhaled sharply. "Nicolò, these are all designer labels. They must have cost the earth."

He shrugged. "That's what you wear. Take back whatever you don't like. You also warned me some of them would need to be altered before they could be worn." He gave her an odd look. "I thought you'd be delighted by a brand-new wardrobe."

Did she sound ungrateful? She bit down on her lip, struggling for something appropriate to say. "Thank you," she managed. "These are all gorgeous."

"And yet . . ." He tilted his head to one side, fixing those unnerving dark eyes on her, eyes that seemed to see straight down into her soul. "I can tell you're less than thrilled."

"It's just a little overwhelming." She spared the closet an uncomfortable glance. "I'll adjust in time," she said, before adding beneath her breath, "Maybe."

So, why the knee-jerk reaction to the unexpected riches? Why did she shrink from the beauty and luxury of what he'd shown her? She couldn't explain it. It just felt wrong, as if she'd fallen into someone else's life and didn't have a clue how to get back to her own.

Nicolò caught her left hand in his and she stilled, overcome by the burn of The Inferno. This she understood. This grounded and centered her. His touch. Her reaction to his touch. That remarkable kiss they'd shared. The need that clawed at her, insisting they complete what they'd started. More than anything she wanted to walk out of this room and into the bedroom she'd once shared with him. Where she belonged.

Before she could put thought to action, he said, "There's one other thing missing."

You, she wanted to say. His mouth on hers. His skin against her skin. Taking her and making her his. "What's missing?"

He lifted her hand. "Your wedding rings."

Her eyes widened in alarm. "Did I lose them in the accident?"

"As I mentioned, our wedding was a spur-of-the-moment affair. We were supposed to buy our rings the day you were injured."

Her brows drew together. "Oh, how sad."

"Don't worry. We'll get it taken care of as soon as you've recovered." He offered a crooked smile. "We'll make a special day of it. How about that?"

She hesitated. "Are you sure you don't want to wait until I get my memory back?"

"I hadn't considered that." Again came his penetrating look. "Do you think you'll change your mind about the style between now and then?"

She spared an uneasy glance toward the closet. "It's possible. Maybe our tastes are formed by our past experiences. I wouldn't want to make any decisions I'll regret later."

"If you change your mind later, we'll simply replace the rings."

"Just like that?" she marveled, before confronting him. "As though they had no meaning? As though one ring is as good as another? Tell me something, Nicolò, is that what you believe? More to the point, is that what I believed?"

He shook his head. "We never discussed it."

"No, of course not. Why would we?" Who could have imagined something like this happening? Or made contingency plans in the event it did. "I'll tell you what, let's stick with something simple. Something along the line of a plain pair of bands. If we change our mind later on, we can choose rings that strike us as more meaningful."

"You don't have to make a decision right now. You never know. You might see something you fall in love with when we go to the shop." He opened the top dresser door and removed a small square box. "Here. This is yours. You were wearing it the day of your accident."

She took the box from him, surprised by the weight of it. Removing the top, she found an intricate silver locket on a matching chain. "It's beautiful." She shot him a hopeful glance. "Did you give this to me?"

"I can't take credit for that, I'm afraid. It's your favorite piece of jewelry. A family heirloom, I believe."

"It does appear old." She turned it over, searching for a hinge. "It looks like it should open, but I don't see how. Do you know?"

He shook his head. "If it opens, you never showed me the secret. If you're curious, we can take it to a jeweler and see if they can figure it out."

"That's a good idea." She held the locket out to him. "Would you mind putting it on?"

He took the necklace and she turned, sweeping her hair aside so he could fasten the chain around her neck. She caught a brief glimpse of herself in the huge antique mirror hanging above the dresser and it gave her a start. From the moment she'd first seen her reflection in the hospital, it never failed to surprise her.

"What is it?" Nicolò asked as he fastened the locket in place.

The instant he finished, she turned her back on her image. "Nothing." She offered a bright smile. "Everything's terrific."

She could tell he didn't buy it. He dropped his hands to her shoulders and forced her to face her reflection once again. "Why do you have so much difficulty looking at yourself?"

"I guess because I see the sort of woman I wish I were." She released a frustrated laugh. "That sounds bizarre, doesn't it?"

"A little." He eased her hair back from her face so it poured down her back. "You don't have to wish to be the woman you see. You are her."

"You don't understand."

His hands tightened on her shoulders, giving them a gentle squeeze. "Then explain it to me."

"This is so frustrating. I don't even remember what I look like. The first time I saw myself in a mirror—"

"It was like looking at a complete stranger?"

"Yes!" She started to swivel around again, but he wouldn't let her. Instead, she met his gaze in the mirror, his midnight black, hers springtime green. "I keep staring at myself, trying to discover some clue to my personality. And the best I can come up with is that I seem . . . nice."

"I'd call you beautiful." He tilted his head. "Part pixie and part angel."

The color deepened in her cheeks, betraying her reaction to his words. "I meant character, as well as appearance. I'm pretty. Maybe even more than pretty. But I look . . ." She stared at herself.

For some reason his expression went blank. "Nice."

She couldn't help grinning. "Yes. Don't misunderstand. That's a good thing. I want to be a nice person. I feel nice." She touched a spot just above her heart, close to where her locket nestled. "Inside."

"Then you must be," he informed her lightly. "Otherwise I wouldn't have married you."

She relaxed within his embrace. "I'm relieved to hear you say it." Then she stiffened as another thought occurred to her. "But what if I've changed because of the amnesia? What if I'm not the same person I was before? What if I turn into a class A bitch or start throwing temper tantrums or pilfering the silver?"

In the mirror, she saw his eyes narrow and it caused her heart to give a small jump. "Are you feeling any larcenous urges?" he asked.

"Not even a little, but—"

"Not a little niggle to stick a silver fork in your back pocket?"

Her lips quivered. "None," she confessed.

"Any urge to throw things or call me foul names?"

The smile forming on her mouth grew. "Not yet."

He dropped a kiss on the top of her head. "Good. Then you don't have anything to worry about."

She turned and this time he didn't try and stop her. Her smile faded. "But, aren't our personalities formed by the events and circumstances of our past? Since I don't have any background notes to draw from—"

"Then you'll have to rely on your instincts and allow yourself to live your life the way that feels right."

Frustration ate at her. "You make it sound so simple."

"It is that simple. Do what feels right inside." He brushed the back of his hand along the curve of her cheek. "Why don't you rest and I'll order up some dinner."

For some reason, that amused her, which helped break the tension. "I gather you don't cook?"

"I can manage toast, if forced. I leave the kitchen to experts like Marco and my grandfather."

"Marco's a brother?" she guessed.

"One of three older brothers." He ticked off on his fingers. "Sev, the eldest. Then there's Marco and Lazz, who are twins. We were raised by my grandparents, Primo and Nonna. Then there's a slew of cousins and the odd sister-in-law or two."

A sudden thought struck and she couldn't believe it hadn't occurred to her before this. "What about me?" she asked eagerly. "Do I have any relatives?"

He shook his head. "You don't have any brothers or sisters, and your father died when you were a baby. Your mother's still around, but I haven't been able to locate her. Don't panic," he added, when she started to do just that. "According to what you've told me, it's not unusual for her to take off for weeks at a time. You said she travels a lot."

Her excitement dimmed, replaced by dismay. So she really did have no one. Or next to no one. "It doesn't sound as though I have a very close relationship with my mother, if I lose track of her for weeks on end."

Imagine if she'd never met Nicolò. If they'd never fallen in love and married. She'd have been utterly alone dealing with the aftermath of her accident, with no memory and no family to help her. She shivered in distress. He must have read her thoughts, or maybe they were mirrored on her face.

"You have my family," he told her gruffly, "even if I haven't had an opportunity to introduce you to everyone."

"Our relationship developed that fast?" she asked uneasily.

"You're looking worried again. Don't be. There'll be plenty of time to meet them once you've had a chance to recover."

"And if I don't recover?" she asked, tension underscoring the question.

He smiled. "Since you never met any of them before, it'll be a new experience for both old and new Kiley."

"Huh." The concept intrigued her. "Old and new. That's an interesting way to look at it."

Nicolò frowned in concern. "You're exhausted, aren't you? And I can tell just looking at you that your headache has started up again. Probably from all the worrying." He nudged her in the direction of the bed. "Get some sleep. I'll be close by if you need me."

Without thought, Kiley lifted her mouth for his kiss, only a split second later realizing what she'd done. She caught a momentary glimpse of something dart through his gaze, a hint of surprise mingling with an intense desire. And then his head dipped downward.

Before, in the hospital, he'd consumed her, his need a hard, driven thing. This time the kiss came softly, leisurely, but no less powerful for all that. She shuddered within his hold, reveling in the hot spice of his kiss, as swept away this time as she'd been the first.

He tugged her closer, exploring the curves of her body as he deepened their kiss. He cupped her breasts through the knit material of her shirt, thumbing the tips until they tightened into hard, rigid peaks. Before she could do more than gasp in reaction, he slipped beneath her knit shirt to investigate further.

His hands spread across the narrow expanse of her waist and the inch of sensitive skin between the gap of shirt and jeans before finding her breasts again. He teased them through her bra, the slide of the thin silk across the aching peaks almost more than she could stand. He must have realized as much because he dragged his fingertips in a torturous path to her hips, his fingers just curving around her flanks.

She could feel his erection surging against her belly and his mouth grew more determined, driving instead of teasing. His hands began to move again, restlessly exploring the curve of her backside, lightly tracing the flare of her hips before sliding to cup her where her need burned hottest. She wanted him. Heaven help her, but she wanted him to rip away her clothes and spread her on the bed behind them and give her the relief her body wept for.

She sensed he hovered on the very edge of control. They teetered there for an endless moment, locked together, on the verge of taking that final, irrevocable step. At the last instant, he released her and stepped back. But it cost him, his expression drawn into taut lines of pain.

"Sleep," he told her, the single word shredded almost beyond recognition. "You need sleep far more than this."

Kiley would have argued, but exhaustion fell over her like a blanket and she did as he suggested, curling up on top of the bed. If she'd had any doubts about their relationship, Nicolò had put them to rest in the past few minutes. How was it possible that it only took one touch from the man? A single touch and she melted in mindless desire. No way would she do that unless on some level she recognized and trusted him.

She smiled sleepily. He had a knack for easing her fears, helping her to deal with her memory loss. She doubted she'd have been able to get through this if she'd been on her own. But with her husband by her side, she felt she could tackle just about any adversity. She yawned.

How had she gotten so lucky?

The sound of gunshots woke Nicolò and sent him leaping from the bed and racing into the hallway. It was only then he realized the noise came from the downstairs TV. After checking Kiley's room and finding it empty, he headed for the steps, surprised to discover every light in the house ablaze. He followed the trail of lights to the kitchen, turning them off as he progressed through the house.

Earlier, he'd planned to wake Kiley when their dinner arrived. But he'd found her sleeping so soundly, he didn't have the heart to disturb her. Leaving a note seemed the best option, and it had worked, since a quick check of the refrigerator told him that she'd polished off the Chinese leftovers. He was less pleased to discover Brutus had cleaned out everything else. Greedy mutt. It would seem this new version of Kiley was an easy touch, and Brutus sensed as much.

Next, he turned off the trail of lights leading through the dining room, into the living room and finally to the den. And that's where he found her. She and Brutus were curled up together on his couch, both sound asleep and utterly oblivious to the raging gunfight from a 40s gangster movie playing on the television.

She'd donned one of the nightgowns and robes he'd bought during her hospital stay, the robin's egg-blue setting off the vividness of her hair and the creamy paleness of her skin. She'd forked her fingers deep into Brutus's coat, her hand fine-boned and delicate against the huge, muscular dog. Brutus lay curled protectively around her, his breath escaping in deep, rumbling snores.

The desire Nicolò had felt earlier came storming back, just as messy and uncontrollable and incomprehensible as before. He hesitated, no more than an inch away from ripping off her nightgown and covering her body with his own. She wouldn't resist. Hell, based on her reaction a few scant hours ago, she'd open to him as sweetly now as she'd done then. He took a single step in her direction before he caught the violent purple bruising along the back of her shoulder.

He sucked in a shuddering breath and crossed to turn off the television, which instantly woke Kiley. Or maybe it was his lifting her in his arms that disturbed her slumber. He carried her from the room, much to the annoyance of a disgruntled Brutus.

"Where are we going?" she asked, wrapping her arms around Nicolò's neck and yawning broadly.

Her scent drifted to him, light and feminine and unmistakably her own. "Back to bed," he answered her question.

"Oh." She wrinkled her nose. "I'd really rather not."

That gave him pause. "You prefer sleeping with my dog?"

She hesitated, a heart-wrenching vulnerability sweeping across her face and shadowing her eyes. Nicolò found it difficult to believe she could fake the expression, especially straight out of a sound sleep. But perhaps he wasn't the best judge. At least, not right here and now.

"I'd rather not sleep alone," she confessed. "It's not that I'm afraid. Not exactly. It's just I don't like being by myself. I'm not used to it."

"I can solve that problem for you."

It was inevitable. It had been from the minute he'd first seen her. First touched her. First claimed her as his own. One way or another she was destined to end up in his bed. Better sooner than later.

"Are you taking me to our bedroom?"

"Yes."

"Will you sleep with me?"

"Without question." Even if it meant an eternity of hellfire and damnation.

She snuggled deeper into his hold. "That's okay then."

Nicolò shouldered through the door to his bedroom suite and crossed to the bed. He deposited her there, struck by how small and fragile she appeared curled up on his king-sized mattress. Maybe that's how she succeeded with her cons, by looking so utterly innocent. She blinked sleepily up at him and smiled.

"Aren't you coming back to bed?" she asked.

"I am. Although, now that I have you here . . ." He tilted his head to one side and studied her. "What will I do with you?"

Chapter Four

"*I can tell you* exactly what you should do with me," Kiley replied.

Desire flashed through Nicolò. "And what's that?"

Unable to resist, he joined her in the bed and scooped her close, cushioning her head against his shoulder. There was something different about her, he realized. A quality that hadn't been there when they'd first met, as well as a quality that had vanished as completely as her memory. And then it hit him.

The cunning he'd seen in that other version of Kiley was missing. And in its place sparkled kindness and generosity and an openness he suspected would have been utterly foreign to her nature only a few short days ago.

Of course, it could all be an act, a brilliant charade to keep him off balance. But if she were faking amnesia, he was absolutely certain he'd have caught her "tell," just as he had in the hotel room during their first confrontation. He'd have noticed some small indication of subterfuge. So far there had been none.

She curled into his embrace, fitting her curves to his angles as though it were the most natural thing in the world. As though they'd slept like this a thousand times before. For an instant they both stilled, and Nicolò became intensely aware of the intimacy of their position. He could hear her slow, shallow breathing and feel the slide of silk against his side, along with the pressure of her small, rounded breasts. Cautiously, her hand crept across his chest settling just above his heart.

More than anything, he wanted to flip her onto her back and fill her to overflowing, to take her with mouth and body. To join with her in that ultimate dance of pleasure. Nothing mattered except that he have her here and now, in his arms. He'd worry about the ramifications of his actions later. When Juice turned in his report proving Kiley's guilt. When Kiley regained her memory. When all his outrageous mistakes hit the fan, he'd find a way around it. Because that's what he did. That's what he'd always done. In the meantime, why shouldn't they enjoy what fate had so generously provided? He should take the offering and enjoy it to the fullest, and to hell with the consequences.

But he couldn't. She'd only been released from the hospital mere hours ago, he reminded himself. She had bruises on top of bruises. And most damning of all . . .

She was a con artist.

It didn't matter that The Inferno shrieked through him, clawing at him to take that final step of possession. It didn't matter that Kiley seemed equally inclined to make the ultimate commitment. He couldn't trust this woman, didn't dare believe that any of this was real. He'd put his family's well-being at risk if he fell for her game. Though right this minute he almost— *almost*— didn't give a damn.

She stroked her fingertips across his chest in tiny, tantalizing circles. "I know exactly what you should do with me," she repeated. "It occurred to me while I was downstairs." The softest laugh escaped her, her breath caressing his chin and neck and wreaking havoc with his self-control. "I'd like to start over."

Okay, not quite what he'd expected. He caught her hand in his before he lost it completely. "Start over," he repeated.

She nodded, eagerness brightening her eyes. "It occurred to me when I was getting reacquainted with Brutus. You see, I don't remember any of my previous interactions with him."

Maybe because there hadn't been any. The only reason Brutus had recognized her scent when he'd first introduced them was because he'd allowed the dog to sniff some of her possessions after he'd had them transferred into his house. "When your memory returns, all that will be resolved," Nicolò offered. Of course, when her memory returned, he'd be the one in the doghouse.

"No. I can't wait for that. I have to live my life now." She regarded him in all seriousness. "I don't remember any of my interactions with Brutus, any more than I remember our interactions. I can't ask Brutus what happened."

He found himself giving her back a sympathetic stroke. "But you can ask me."

Determination filled her expression, and perhaps a hint of desperation, as well. "I want to do more than ask. And that's where my idea comes in."

He needed to stop touching her and soon. But even as the thought dawned, Nicolò found himself tucking a strand of her hair behind her ear, his fingers lingering on the silky curve of her cheek. "Tell me your idea."

"You said ours was a whirlwind affair." She waited for his nod of confirmation before continuing. "So that means it wouldn't be too difficult to reenact, right?"

Aw, hell. "Reenact, as in create all over again?" he asked.

She smiled and he suddenly realized that her smile was a tiny bit crooked, her lips tugging ever so slightly to the right. For some odd reason, he found the imperfection all too appealing. "Exactly. We can recreate our first meeting, and each of our subsequent dates. Best of all, maybe it'll help me remember."

Actually, it was a very clever idea, one that would provide her with endless amusement if she were faking amnesia. Considering they didn't have a history, other than that one disastrous meeting at Le Premier, he'd find it impossible to come up with anything real, which left creating some ridiculous fantasy.

Everything within him flinched from the idea. He'd been dishonest enough by claiming her as his wife. Granted, The Inferno had united him with this woman, and perhaps if circumstances had been different he might have pursued a serious relationship in order to see where it might take them. But no way in hell would he permanently connect himself with a con artist.

The reminder of who and what she was stiffened his resolve. He'd put this game in motion for a reason. A very simple, extremely vital reason. If Kiley O'Dell succeeded with her scam, she could conceivably claim half the value of the fire diamond mine and the Dante family jewelry empire would go under. He had to play out this game until he had proof of her true nature. Unfortunately, his physical reaction to her complicated matters.

"Nicolò?" She looked far less excited than moments before. "What's wrong? Don't you like my idea?"

"I love your idea."

"Then will you do it?"

He was digging himself deeper and deeper into an inescapable hole. How would he justify his actions if Juice proved her innocence? He couldn't. And when she recovered her memory, those actions would cause her unfathomable pain.

But then, he didn't believe for one minute she was an innocent in all this, not based on her actions and attitude that day at Le Premier. That woman and the one currently in his arms bore no relationship to each other. Until the two melded together once again, he'd follow the course he'd set for himself. For both of them. In fact, if he played this the way she requested, he might be able to prove what she was, as well as the truth behind her claim of amnesia.

"Yes, I'll do it," he agreed. "We'll start all over again."

He could feel her relief. "Where did we first meet?"

"In the park," he answered promptly, following the history he'd scripted in anticipation of this conversation. "I was walking Brutus."

"And what was I doing there?"

"Sitting. You'd just moved to the city in order to begin a new job. Unfortunately, the company folded the week after you started."

"You took pity on me, didn't you?"

The fantasy she'd created to fill in the holes in her memory showed an impressive ingenuity and amazed the hell out of him. Unfortunately, the warmth with which she regarded him left him stirring in discomfort.

"Brutus and I both did," he said, forcing out the lie. "We cheered you up with a rousing game of Frisbee."

"Then tomorrow that's what we'll do. We'll go to the park and play Frisbee."

"Actually, we won't."

"But—"

He shook his head. "You're less than a day out of the hospital. We're not doing anything that risks putting you back there again. Frisbee is out." When she would have argued further, he added, "It was just a brief encounter, Kiley. I have an alternate suggestion, if you're willing."

"Which is?"

"I'll recreate our times together, if that's how you want to play the game." And this very well could be a game for her, he reminded himself. "In return, you don't ask any questions beforehand. Let events unfold naturally."

"I don't understand. Why?"

"Because this way you don't have any preconceived expectations. You can just be yourself and enjoy the occasion. There won't be any 'did I do this' or 'did I say that?' You can just take it as it happens and respond naturally."

"But I don't know what's natural for me," she argued.

"Then go with what feels right."

She hesitated, considering, before giving a reluctant nod. "I guess I can do that. Are you sure we can't start tomorrow?"

He shook his head. "We wait until the doctor clears you for normal activity."

She grinned, her mouth taking on that lopsided slant again. "In that case, I'll call Ruiz first thing tomorrow."

Nicolò considered for a moment, then shrugged. "If he gives you the okay, I'm fine with it. But I'll need a little time to set everything up."

And the first thing he'd set up would be a few "dates" that would help him determine whether or not she truly had amnesia, while giving Juice additional time to complete his background check. Dates that would prove she was a woman who craved the good life and all the expensive accessories that went with it. Until then . . .

He stretched out his arm and flicked off the light. "Try and sleep." Because heaven knew, he wouldn't. Not with her in his bed, wrapped around him, while he couldn't do more than plant a chaste kiss on her brow.

She stirred against him, threatening to shred his ability for any sort of chaste embrace. Or so he thought until she said, "I—I don't like it this dark."

"I'm right here," he said, reassuring her. "I won't let anything happen to you. But if you'd be more comfortable with the light on . . ." He reached for the lamp again. "Better?"

"Do you mind?" Her eyes turned so shadowed they were almost as black as his own. "Ever since the accident—"

"What?" He threaded his fingers through her hair, careful to avoid the stitches from her injury. "Do you remember something?"

"No, it's not that." She moistened her lips. "As long as I can remember—which, granted, isn't long—it's never been this dark or so quiet. Hospitals are noisy, busy places. Until I woke up in your guest bedroom, I don't ever remember being alone before. I didn't like it."

It took him a moment to reply. "There's an easy fix to that. From now on, you sleep here with me and we leave a light on."

A hint of uncertainty swept across her expressive features. "Are you sure you don't mind?"

"Not even a little."

He continued to hold her until she drifted off, calling himself six kinds of fool. He watched as she slept, memorizing every curve and angle of her face. She was out cold, no faking that, so relaxed and trusting within his embrace.

She'd regained some of her color, her cheeks carrying a light flush instead of that frightening waxy pallor she'd worn during her hospital visit. And her hair fell in heavy curls across her shoulders and his bared chest, the soft, springy feel of it sheer torture.

Her lips were parted ever so slightly, making him long to sample them again, to delve inward and invade that honeyed warmth. To see if she tasted as sweet and rich as before or if he'd imagined it.

How could someone who looked so innocent be so amoral? Every instinct he possessed insisted she was telling the truth. That her amnesia was real. If he only had himself to consider, he'd take the risk. But his responsibilities encompassed far more than himself, and that meant he needed to use extreme caution. He had to remain on his guard every second, especially during moments like these. Intimate, private, vulnerable moments that someone experienced in running a con could turn to her advantage.

He closed his eyes, wishing he had the ability to trust. Wishing that he could believe in things like The Inferno and second chances and the goodness of human nature. But in his capacity as Dantes' troubleshooter he'd experienced far too much of the opposite to ever take such a leap of faith.

Even as the thought lingered in his mind, he settled her more firmly within his hold, his embrace equal parts possessive and protective. And as he joined her in sleep, one word sounded louder than all the others.

Mine.

Three endless days passed before Kiley received the official okay from Dr. Ruiz to resume normal activities. He also gave her the name of a doctor who specialized in retrograde amnesia, though she hoped she wouldn't need his services. Instead, she preferred to trust that with her husband's help, her memory would return on its own. It was just a matter of when.

She wished she could explain how disoriented she felt. Nicolò knew everything about her, while she knew nothing. Nothing about herself. Nothing about her likes and dislikes. Nothing about her personality or hopes or dreams. It put her in a position of reacting to all that went on around her instead of driving or controlling events. It also forced her to trust implicitly, which filled her with uncertainty and fear.

Every aspect of her life ended in a giant question mark. And every time she had to ask a question about herself and the appropriateness of her actions, or about mist-shrouded events from her past, or unremembered plans for her future, it left her both dependent and vulnerable.

Well, at least she could state two things with absolute certainty. First, she didn't like feeling either dependent or vulnerable. So, with each day that passed, she intended to make strides to put some distance between herself and those particular characteristics. To find a way to win back control over her life.

And second, despite her inability to recall the details of her previous life, her feelings toward her husband hadn't changed. It offered untold relief she felt such a powerful hunger toward the man at her side. That she couldn't wait to be with him, held safe within his arms. To kiss him again. To relive that joy of loving and being loved. And to uncover all the secrets he kept hidden from the rest of the world, secrets he'd probably shared with her, and her alone, if only she could remember.

She wanted him. Needed him. And she had little doubt that they'd act on those desires before very much longer. Soon she'd experience anew those soul-stirring emotions when he made love to her for the first time. Maybe in those intensely intimate moments her memory would return.

She could only hope.

"I'm sure everything will come back to me if we recreate our dates," she told Nicolò. "It's bound to spark something, right?"

"It's quite possible."

Her enthusiasm dimmed. "Do you think the fact I haven't had any flashes of recall so far means it won't return?"

He instantly wrapped his arms around her. "Not at all. And now that you've been given the all-clear, we'll see what memories we can shake loose."

They decided to skip their first meeting in the park and move on to their first "real" date. To Kiley's dismay, it didn't go quite the way she'd hoped. The day started off well enough. Her excitement at their implementing her plan carried her through the first couple hours as they toured the delights of San Francisco.

Nicolò took her to all the top tourist spots—Fisherman's Wharf and Ghirardelli Square with its view of Alcatraz Island, for a ride on the cable cars that rumbled through Chinatown and past Lombard Street, topped with a drive through Golden Gate Park. It was an exhausting array of sights and sounds, odors and impressions. Unfortunately, not one place incited more than a faint glimmer of recognition in the murky recesses of her mind, an awareness she'd read about or seen pictures of the city at some point.

And with every stop, she glanced toward Nicolò, hoping against hope to gain some clue as to that first time. Despite her promise to him, she wanted to ask if this occasion matched the one from the past. Had they said the same things? Had they laughed or talked or shared confidences then, all the important tidbits they weren't sharing this time around because she was too empty to have anything worth contributing?

Eventually, he became aware of her growing silence and sideways looks. "What's wrong?" he asked.

She collapsed on a park bench with a weary sigh. "This isn't working quite the way I'd thought it would."

He joined her on the bench. "You don't remember anything? Not necessarily our time together, but I hoped you might remember one of the places we've been. That it might spark some vague memory."

She shook her head, frustrated beyond belief. "I don't remember a blessed thing," she confessed. "Not any of the tourist spots." She spared him a swift, reluctant glance. "Not being with you. Ever."

He lowered his head. "I'm sorry, Kiley."

She covered his hand with hers. "None of this is your fault." He opened his mouth to argue and she cut him off. "I know you want to take responsibility for my accident. But you have to admit that if I'd been less impulsive, I wouldn't have been in the middle of a busy intersection where I could be hit by a cab."

She watched him struggle with that for a moment. "Why don't we agree to disagree on that particular subject?" he suggested with a grim smile.

Her return smile attempted to tease away his seriousness. "I can live with that." His hand tightened on hers, tugging her close. She slid into his hold with the ease of familiarity and tilted her head to one side in consideration. "What next? Do we continue with our tour? Or can you think of something else that might help me remember?"

He hesitated, before nodding. "There's one more place that might prompt a memory."

"And where's that?"

He gave her the sort of grin that threatened to melt her bones. No doubt it was the same smile he'd used during those earlier dates, if only she could recall. All he had to do was switch it on her and she could feel everything soft and feminine surrendering to him, softening, urging her to agree to anything he might ask of her.

"Come on. I'd rather it be a surprise."

He drove them from the park into the heart of the city toward the financial district and Embarcadero. Beneath one of the towering skyscrapers, he pulled into an underground parking lot and escorted her to a private elevator that shot them straight to a penthouse suite. When the doors parted, they stepped out into a massive room, which at first glance appeared to be someone's private residence.

Kiley entered ahead of Nicolò, sinking into the thick, plush carpet, the soft dove-gray color lending the area an opulent, yet intimate feel. There were several divans decorated in a subtle pinstripe of gray and white, accented with a narrow band of black, and silk chairs in a rich ruby red. The pieces were simple, yet exquisite.

Glass tables were arranged in front of the divans and chairs, sitting slightly higher than conventional coffee tables. The lighting also struck her as different, overhead spots creating blazing puddles of brilliance that struck the various tables, while the seats remained in soft shadow. Plants and elaborate fresh flower arrangements gave the area an added warmth.

"What is this place?" she whispered.

"Dantes Exclusive." Was it her imagination or did his gaze grow as intense as the spotlights?

"Dantes? I don't . . ." She shook her head in confusion. "Is this your family business?"

"You haven't heard of Dantes?"

She blinked. "Are you talking about the jewelry firm?" He simply continued to watch her and her breath escaped in a soft gasp. "You're one of *those* Dantes?"

"You remember us?"

She regarded him uneasily, regarding her husband in an entirely different light. She'd sensed his power, witnessed his affluence. But it never occurred to her that he moved in such elite circles. Or that she did. How could she possibly live up to what would be expected of a Dante wife?

"I wouldn't say I remember, exactly," she finally responded. "I know about Dantes the same way I know who the current president is. I retain general knowledge, just not specific memories about my past. I've heard of Dantes. I mean, who hasn't?"

He appeared to accept her comment at face value, though it troubled her he continued to question her amnesia. She kept feeling as though he was concealing something from her. Was it something he hoped she'd remember? Or something he preferred remain forgotten?

"Dantes Exclusive is the part of our retail operation for our high-end clients. It's by appointment only. I thought you might enjoy seeing some of our more select designs."

She managed a smile. Had he sprung this on her last time? Is that why he'd brought her here, today? "I'd enjoy that. Thank you."

He led her through the sitting area, past an impressive glass-and-mirror wet bar offering every possible libation, to a barely visible door set into the wall and protected by an elaborate security system. Nicolò removed a card from his wallet and swiped it across the device, before unlocking the mechanism with a combination of voice and thumbprint. The door clicked open and he escorted Kiley into a glittering fantasyland.

She stared around, wide-eyed. "Oh," she managed to murmur.

"Feel free to look around while I see if any of the family's here."

She looked at him in alarm. "Your family?"

"Don't panic. They won't hurt you. I promise." He started to leave, then hesitated. "Unless you want to be hermetically sealed in here, I'd look but not touch."

Kiley whipped her hands behind her back and interlaced her fingers. "I wouldn't dream of touching."

The minute he disappeared, she made a slow circuit of the room, feeling more overwhelmed with each step she took. Case after case displayed jewelry sets of stunning beauty. Not to mention astronomical expense. Is this the world to which she belonged? She shook her head. No, it didn't feel right. Surely, she didn't live a life of such wealth and opulence.

She paused in front of a particularly gorgeous display. Voices drifted to her from the doorway through which her husband had vanished. Nicolò's low murmur sent awareness rippling down her spine. Then came the higher-pitched reply of a woman. At first Kiley couldn't hear the actual words, but the contentious intonation came through loud and clear. Then the woman raised her voice.

"Forget it, Nicolò," she said. "I won't be party to—"

Nicolò interrupted, speaking at length in a soft, hard voice.

Then, "Okay, fine. But this is the one and only time."

Kiley hastened away from the doorway, worry balled in the pit of her stomach. What in the world did Nicolò want, and why wouldn't the woman he spoke to be party to whatever he'd suggested? Of even more concern, did their conversation involve her?

She paused by another display case, focusing all her attention on the glorious necklace, earrings, and bracelet. She was enthralled by their stunning appeal, despite her apprehension. A moment later, Nicolò entered the room, followed by a tall, elegant blonde with dark eyes. She offered a forced smile that left Kiley feeling intensely uncomfortable.

"This is my sister-in-law, Francesca," Nicolò said. "She's Sev's wife and Dantes' top designer. You're looking at one of her designs."

"It's incredible," Kiley said as they shook hands. "Simple, yet elegant. And—and warm."

Her utter sincerity must have come through because Francesca's smile softened and the cool wariness eased from her gaze. "Thank you. It's part of a collection I created called Dante's Heart."

Kiley turned back to study the display case. "I think it's my favorite of all the ones I've seen here today."

"It's the fire diamonds," Francesca stated. "Working with them makes even the most ordinary piece extraordinary."

"Is that what you call those particular diamonds?" Kiley peered closer. "Oh, wow. I see it now. It is almost as though they're on fire."

She didn't know what alerted her. Perhaps it was the fierce stillness emanating from Francesca and Nicolò. Or perhaps she felt the intensity of their joint gaze. Kiley glanced up at them and slowly straightened.

"Could you please tell me what's going on?" she asked. "It's bad enough that I don't remember. But I also don't understand the silent subtext between you two." She focused on Nicolò. "Is there some reason I'm here other than your wanting to show me the family business and introduce me to Francesca?"

"I was hoping that seeing the fire diamonds might prompt a memory."

"What memory?"

"Any memory." He tilted his head to one side. "But it doesn't, does it?"

"Not even a little." She offered a strained smile. "I wish I had your talent, Francesca. It must give you such pleasure to create these spectacular—" And then a possibility struck her, one that left her trembling with excitement. "Oh, my God. Am I a jewelry designer, too? Is that why I'm here? Is that why you're acting so strangely? Am I supposed to recognize something I created?"

Struggling to contain a wild thrill of hope, she looked around with a hint of desperation before darting toward a wall full of display cases. She scanned them swiftly, praying that one of the sets would jump out and connect with her the same way she'd connected with Nicolò.

"I don't recognize anything. I'm trying. Really I am, but—" She glanced over her shoulder, her gaze clashing with Nicolò's. "Please. *Please* help me."

He reached her side before she'd even finished speaking and wrapped her up in a tight embrace. "Hell. I'm sorry, sweetheart." He held her close, comforting her with his warmth. "It's nothing like that."

"Oh." Kiley struggled to conceal the magnitude of her disappointment, praying she could blink back the tears before he saw them. She might have hidden them from Nicolò, but she had less luck with Francesca.

The other woman joined them and caught Kiley's hand in hers. "I am *so* sorry," Francesca said. "It didn't occur to me that you'd jump to that conclusion. Though now that you have, it seems such an obvious leap to make. I can't apologize enough for being so cruel."

"Don't—" Kiley could feel her emotions escaping her control. She waved a hand in front of her face. "Ignore me. I probably overdid today and it's all caught up with me at once."

"Nicolò," Francesca whispered fiercely, more than a hint of anger coloring her voice.

"This is my fault," he replied. "I'll deal with it."

He glanced down at Kiley. One look at her face had him swearing beneath his breath. She buried her face against the front of his shirt and he jerked his head at Francesca, who left without a word, though her infuriated expression spoke volumes.

"I'm sorry," he said. "I really screwed this up. I meant for you to look at some of the wedding ring sets and see if anything appealed."

"It's too much, Nicolò. Too overwhelming and way too soon."

"I realize that." He grimaced. "At least, I realize that now."

"Should I assume that our first date didn't end like this?" she asked in a muffled voice.

"With you in tears? No, it didn't, thank God."

She released a watery laugh. "I'm relieved to hear it." She peeked up at him. "Just out of curiosity, how did it end?"

He closed his eyes, fighting an inner battle. A losing inner battle. "Like this . . ."

Chapter Five

He cupped her face, lifted it to his, and kissed her. She tasted of sweetness and tears, heat and hope, all mixed with white-hot desire. He shouldn't touch her. He sure as hell shouldn't kiss her. He'd thought by bringing her here, to the heart of Dantes' wealth and power, he'd catch a glimpse of something. Avarice. Delight. A quick hungry look she couldn't quite conceal.

But she hadn't shown a bit of that, not even after he'd left her alone in the room and watched her on the close-circuit cameras. If anything, she'd appeared nervous and uncomfortable, as though she'd rather have been almost anywhere other than stuck in a room with countless millions of dollars' worth of the world's most stunning jewelry.

She melted against him, her mouth parting beneath his. Unable to resist, he dipped inward. The flames from The Inferno roared to life, raging through him like wildfire. If they'd been anywhere else, he'd have said to hell with it and taken her right there and then. And based on the way she clung to him, wrapped herself around him, opened to him without hesitation, she wouldn't have lifted a finger to stop him.

"I'd like to see you in one of these designs," he told her between kisses. "Clothed in fire diamonds and black satin sheets."

She shivered against him. "That would still leave too much between us. Let's skip the diamonds and sheets. I'd rather be clothed in Dante. Or at least, one particular Dante."

"Much as I'd like to accommodate you, we can't. Not until you've had time to heal. Until then," He snatched another deep, penetrating kiss. "Let's go home."

Disappointment filled her, despite knowing he was being sensible. Cautious. Right now, she preferred reckless and passionate.

"Home it is," she reluctantly agreed. Though she remained tucked close by his side, she didn't speak again until they were in the elevator, returning to the underground garage. "So, what's your plan for tomorrow?"

An excellent question. Based on Francesca's reaction, he realized he needed to take Kiley away from San Francisco for a short time. Just long enough for Juice to complete his investigation. It would involve a quick phone call to an old family friend, Joc Arnaud. But

Nicolò didn't anticipate any problems from that end of things.

The Dantes and the billionaire financier had enjoyed a long-term friendship. They'd even designed his wife's wedding rings, as well as the jewelry set Joc had presented to Rosalyn on the birth of their son, Joshua. With luck, he'd assist Nicolò now, allowing him to stay on Joc's private island, Isla de los Deseos, while Nicolò decided how to handle the disastrous situation he'd created.

He pulled out of the garage, sparing Kiley a swift glance. She looked pale and exhausted. He'd pushed too hard today and could kick himself for his stupidity. "I have to call a friend in order to set something up. Fair warning, it might take a day or two."

"Is this another of our dates?"

He forced out the lie. "It preceded our marriage. In fact, it was what convinced you to marry me."

"You convinced me to marry you on our second date?"

"No. After today's disaster, I've decided to move our agenda forward a few weeks."

"A few weeks?" she repeated faintly. "You weren't kidding about our having a whirlwind affair, were you?"

"I did warn you that we didn't know each other very long."

She leaned back against the headrest and closed her eyes. "How strange. I must have been an impulsive person. Which explains the dash to beat out a cab."

"That explains you," he muttered. "Now try and explain me."

"I guess we have to blame it on The Inferno. It does seem to have a rather strong effect." She opened her eyes long enough to shoot him a look brimming with laughter. "On both of us."

"No question about that," he agreed.

She was right. The Inferno did have a strong effect on both of them. It also created a dozen problems. How did he put an end to the physical need clawing at him? Because when Juice found the evidence of Kiley's guilt, he'd have to put an end to their relationship. He couldn't—*wouldn't*—join himself with a woman he didn't trust. Not that it would be a problem. As soon as she regained her memory and discovered how he'd scammed her in return, she'd pour ice water on any remaining embers.

And if she didn't regain her memory? He refused to consider the possibility. It would come back. He didn't doubt it for a minute. And when it did, he'd watch a woman with a nature full of sweet generosity transform into a sly, devious creature who made a living by her wits and dishonesty. Perhaps that would put a rapid end to The Inferno.

He could only hope.

Kiley could barely contain her excitement when two days later Nicolò escorted her onto Dantes' corporate jet.

"Where are we going?" she demanded.

He regarded her with a lazy smile that made her long for them to be back in bed where maybe—just maybe—he'd surrender to the passion scorching them both with its relentless flames. So far that hadn't happened. He'd shown a disgusting amount of self-control, determined to wait until the right time and place before making love to her. She didn't have a clue when or where that might occur. As far as she was concerned, here and now would do just fine.

"We're going to Isla de los Deseos," he informed her.

Her tongue savored the syllables. "What a romantic name. What did we do there?"

As expected, he shook his head. "Not a chance. We're going to relax and enjoy ourselves. Nothing strenuous. Nothing that will wear you out. This will give you the opportunity to recoup from your accident. Plus, we'll have the time and privacy we need to get to know each other better."

"We'll also get to reenact the dates that led up to our marriage." She nodded sagely. "I have to hand it to you, Nicolò. Recoup, reacquaint, and reenact. Not many are so adept at killing three birds with one stone."

"Four, but who's counting."

She tilted her head to one side, intrigued. "What's the fourth?"

His eyes grew uncomfortably direct. "Recover. As in, your memory."

"Oh, right."

For some reason that put a damper on her spirits. She didn't understand it. She wanted to recover her memory, didn't she? So, why shy away from the mere suggestion? Part came from a vague impression she picked up from Nicolò, as though he knew more than he'd told her.

No doubt there was. And no doubt when the time was right and she could handle the information, both physically and emotionally, he'd tell her whatever dark secrets he kept locked away. In the meantime, no matter how difficult she found it, she'd have to remain patient and wait until he felt comfortable sharing the information.

She slept for long periods of the flight to Deseos, wrapped in Nicolò's arms, held safe and secure. The rest of the time, they talked, their conversation quiet and intimate. He discussed his past while kneading his palm in an unconscious gesture, explained how he'd been taken in by his grandparents after the sailing accident that had claimed the lives of his mother and father. He spoke of Sev and how hard his eldest brother had worked to recover the family fortunes. He told her about the twins, Marco, the passionate charmer, who had tricked his bride into marriage by pretending to be his twin brother, and Lazz, the analytical loner. And he described his grandparents, how after The Inferno struck, Nonna had broken her engagement to another man and emigrated to California with Nicolò's grandfather, Primo.

She could picture Nicolò so clearly as a youth. Feel his pain. Sense his determination to solve the unsolvable, perhaps as a result of being unable to ease his family's sorrow after his parents' death. She suspected he possessed that same determination to fix her situation. The thought brought a misty smile to her mouth, a mouth he instantly captured with his own.

"I like it when you smile," he told her.

"You say that so reluctantly," she teased. "Are you afraid I'll use it against you?"

"Would you?"

"Yes." She tightened her arms around his neck. "If it made you kiss me again, I'd use it against you on an hourly basis."

She leaned forward to demonstrate when the flight attendant made an appearance, warning they'd be landing in a few minutes. Kiley released her husband with a disappointed sigh and buckled up just as the plane banked over a lush mountainous island dotting the surface of an aquamarine sea. They landed on a private airstrip and were driven to a secluded cabana sitting within the embrace of a stand of palm trees, steps from a private lagoon.

The cabana took Kiley's breath away. Decorated in vivid colors, typical of the Caribbean, it boasted a bamboo floor and every possible modern convenience. "How long are we staying here?" she asked.

Nicolò shrugged. "As long as we want."

She turned in alarm. "I only packed an overnight bag. I don't have enough clothes."

He shrugged. "Not to worry. They don't wear clothes here." He waited a beat before laughing at her expression. "I'm kidding."

"Thank goodness," she said faintly.

"We can buy anything you need."

Her brows drew together. "That seems rather excessive. If you'd just told me, I'd have been happy to—"

"You won't need much. A couple bathing suits. A couple dresses for the evening. We'll check out the shops in a little while."

First the wardrobe full of designer clothes, then Dantes Exclusive, and now this. She regarded him with a troubled expression. "I need to ask you a question and I'm not quite sure how to phrase it."

"Just be direct," he suggested.

"Are we . . . rich? Or rather, are you?"

"Yes."

So brutally frank. "Was—was I?"

He hesitated before shaking his head. "No."

She nodded in relief. "That makes sense. This feels . . ."

His scrutiny intensified. "What?"

"Different," she admitted with a shrug. Then she brightened. "But considering how short a time we've known each other, perhaps that explains it. I'm probably not accustomed to such a lavish lifestyle."

He turned to face her, folding his arms across his chest. She'd always been aware of his impressive size, especially in comparison with her own. But for some reason his current stance made her even more aware of it than usual. "You know that much about yourself, even though you have amnesia?" he asked.

The softness of the question captured her full attention. "It's not anything I remember," she hastened to explain. "It's a feeling I have. Like I'm out of step. Like this isn't me."

"Not you?" He shook his head. "You seem to be operating under a misapprehension that I need to straighten out. You didn't have much money, but you thoroughly enjoyed the best life had to offer."

She couldn't conceal her shock. "I did?"

"Designer clothes and accessories. Five-star hotels." He caught her hands in his and turned them so she could see the lacquered tips. "Professional manicure and pedicure. An expert hairdresser. They were all part of your lifestyle when we first met."

For some reason his words impacted like a body blow. "I didn't know." Nor did she like hearing the truth. It felt wrong. Unappealing. Superficial. Was that the sort of person she'd been before? "If I was so shallow, why were you attracted to me?" she asked, troubled. "Why would you have married me?"

His fingers interlaced with hers until their palms joined. She could feel the heat from The

Inferno build there, melding them together. "It's been like this from the beginning."

Oh, God. She stared at him in distress. "It's physical? Our entire relationship is based on this Inferno we feel for each other? That's it?"

"Would you like there to be more?"

"Of course!" She searched his expression. "Wouldn't you?"

"My grandparents have been married for five and a half decades. I'm well aware there has to be more to marriage than physical attraction. But that takes time to build."

"How do we build it when I know nothing about my background?" she protested, her distress increasing by the second. "Nothing about my history or experiences? How do we find common ground?"

"We start with this—"

He swept her into his arms and ravished her mouth with a kiss that stole every single thought from her head. Heat bloomed, a messy stream of need lapping through her veins and bringing a flush to cheeks and breasts before settling in the very core of her. He invaded her mouth, teasing her until she couldn't stand it any longer.

She fought back, deepening the kiss so it was his turn to catch fire, his turn to burn. His turn to lose control. She tugged his shirt free of his trousers and swept her hands underneath. The instant she hit skin she slowed, tracking a wayward path across his chest as she gathered all that heat in her palms. And then she dipped lower, over the rock-hard ripple of abs to the belt preventing her from a more intimate exploration. She settled for outlining the thick bulge she found there, cupping him as he'd once cupped her. At the last instant, he caught her hands in his and pulled them away.

"We start with this, the physical," he said, gritting out the words. "And we build on it. Together."

She collapsed against his chest and nodded. What a wonderful word. "Together," she whispered.

He made a visible effort to catch his breath. "And he first thing we're doing together is purchasing the clothes we'll need for our stay here."

Kiley wrinkled her nose at him. "That wasn't quite the togetherness I had in mind."

"It wasn't quite the togetherness I had in mind, either." Wry amusement gathered in his dark eyes. "But it'll have to do until—"

"Until when?" she couldn't resist asking.

She'd never seen Nicolò look so conflicted. "Until your memory returns. Until you can make an informed choice."

Iciness replaced the heat of only moments before. *An informed choice?* What did that mean? And of even greater concern, what had happened between them that prompted him to put that sort of condition on their current relationship? What happened the day of her accident that she no longer remembered?

When she first awoke in the hospital, Nicolò had told her they'd fought moments before she'd been injured. Whatever the cause of the argument, it had been serious enough to send her darting in front of a cab. Serious enough, her husband wouldn't make love to her until she remembered.

Was it also serious enough to end their marriage?

Kiley entered the restaurant, Ambrosia, feeling more awkward and uncomfortable than she could ever remember. Her mouth curved in a wry smile. Not that she had much basis for comparison.

At least her bruises were no longer visible, since in the gown Nicolò purchased, they would have stood out like a neon sign. She skated a hand down the pale green silk molded to her waist, hips and thighs before flaring outward in a short train, and struggled to appear poised and confident. It took every ounce of willpower not to tug at the strapless bodice, one that revealed more than it concealed.

She associated the elegant gown with "Old Kiley," a woman, based on her husband's description, she neither liked nor understood. Maybe that other version of herself enjoyed a life rich in sensual pleasure. The only sensual pleasure this Kiley cared about was the one she found in Nicolò's arms.

But did her preference match his? She searched his stunning profile. He was a Dante. A man who hobnobbed with billionaire financiers and jet-setters. He had a position to maintain. And he'd chosen that other Kiley for his life's mate. He'd been so patient with her, but maybe his patience would soon run out. Maybe he'd brought her here in an effort to change her back into the woman he'd first married.

She worried at another possibility, one that concerned her more than any other. Perhaps he chose her originally because she fit into his world, something no longer true. Without a memory of all the little turns of events that led her to develop into the person he married, she could only base her actions on what felt right. And though it broke her heart to admit it, this current getup felt completely wrong. No matter how hard she struggled to fit in, she simply didn't.

Since the moment she'd awoken in that hospital bed and been claimed by her husband, she'd been forced to rely on her instincts. And those instincts—straight down to the core of her—said she bore no relationship to this glossy woman he'd patchworked together for a dinner date with a fancy billionaire glamour couple.

Perhaps that had been true once upon a time. But not any longer. Not unless she regained her memory and lost her current self. If this version of Kiley wasn't good enough for Nicolò, she had a terrible feeling it doomed their relationship before it ever truly began.

The knowledge hung over her like the sword of Damocles, threatening with one swift plunge of the blade to sunder her from a man The Inferno insisted was her soul mate. A man she knew, deep in her heart of hearts, belonged to her every bit as much as she belonged to him.

Or did he belong to that other Kiley?

The maître d' appeared just then and showed them to a private dining alcove and a few minutes later Joc Arnaud and his wife, Rosalyn, appeared. To Kiley's surprise, Rosalyn proved to be a fellow redhead, although her hair gleamed a deep, rich auburn instead of Kiley's brighter shade. Of equal interest, Joc shared Nicolò's coloring.

The similarity ended there, of course. Rosalyn had the height and curves Kiley lacked and crossed the room with long, ground-eating strides that proclaimed her as comfortable on a Texas cattle ranch as in a ballroom. She stuck out her hand with equal forthrightness.

"I'm Rosalyn Arnaud," she announced. "Pleased to meet you. And this is my husband, Joc."

"Kiley O—Dante. Sorry." She released a quick laugh as they all exchanged handshakes. "I guess I'm still getting used to my name."

"Nicolò told us about your accident." Rosalyn took the seat Joc held for her and dropped her hand over Kiley's, giving it a gentle squeeze. "I'm really sorry you're going through such a difficult time."

"The doctors say I could get my memory back at any time."

"In the meanwhile, it must make it very difficult to take everything in. You must feel so dependent and vulnerable."

"That's exactly how I feel," Kiley confessed. "I don't know what I'd do if it weren't for Nicolò."

"Right." Rosalyn's gaze flashed in his direction and she smiled sweetly. "At least you have a husband who loves you and only has your best interests at heart. Someone you can trust to protect you."

Joc took the menu from their waiter and handed it to his wife. "Here you go, Red. See what trouble you can get into with this."

She shot a grin at Kiley and leaned in. "That means be quiet," she whispered in a voice that could be clearly heard by everyone at the table. "Not that I ever listen."

Kiley laughed. "How did you two meet?" she asked, intrigued by the unmistakable differences in attitude and polish between husband and wife.

"Joc sent some goons to my ranch in a vain attempt to buy it. I stormed his citadel and explained why that wasn't going to happen."

"And then?"

"Then he kidnapped me—"

"I most certainly did not," Joc argued. "I tendered an offer which you accepted with impressive alacrity."

"—and he brought me here and proceeded to seduce me." Rosalyn helped herself to a breadstick. "It was actually quite enjoyable."

"Coming here or being seduced?" Kiley asked.

Everyone laughed and Rosalyn gave Kiley a look of undisguised approval. "Since it resulted in our son, Joshua, I'd have to say that tips the scales ever so slightly toward the whole seduction number. What about you?"

"Oh, I'm hoping for a big seduction number, too." She waited for the laughter to die down again before asking, "How old is your son?"

"Not quite a year and walking already," Joc answered. "That's why we were late. We needed to settle him for the night and he wasn't in any hurry to settle. Then I had to talk Rosalyn into putting on the fancy duds."

"I'd live in jeans if it were up to me," she confessed.

"You don't—" Kiley broke off, searching for a more tactful way to phrase her question. "I assumed—"

"That we always live and dress like this?" Rosalyn shook her head. "Honey, if it were up to me, I'd never attend another fancy shindig for the rest of my natural born days. That's Joc's thing, not mine."

"A consequence of my position, I'm afraid." Joc glanced at Nicolò. "And of being a Dante, too, I presume."

Nicolò nodded and it wasn't until then that Kiley became aware of how quiet he'd remained all this time, content to sit back and observe. Observe her, she suddenly realized, while kneading his palm in a gesture that grew more habitual with each passing day.

"I'm not on the frontline quite as much as Sev or the twins," Nicolò conceded. "But I'm forced to do my fair share when the occasion demands."

"I doubt I'll ever get used to it," Kiley confessed. "I'm a nervous wreck right now."

Joc's brows pulled together. "Well, we can fix that easily enough." He shoved back his chair and stood. "I'll arrange for dinner to be delivered to our cabana. You and Nicolò can meet us there in say—" he twitched back a snowy cuff and checked his watch "—twenty minutes? Will that give you time to change into something casual? We'll send the nanny on her way and just relax and eat and have some wine. How does that sound?"

Before Kiley could interject, Nicolò nodded. "Sounds perfect, Joc. Thanks for understanding."

"Nothing to understand," he assured.

They met up twenty minutes later and Kiley thoroughly enjoyed every second of the evening from that point on. After dinner, a demanding wail sounded from one of the bedrooms and a few minutes later Rosalyn appeared with a sleepy baby held close in her arms. At first glance his hair seemed as dark as his father's, but as the two drew closer, Kiley saw it reflected a hint of Rosalyn's deep auburn. He'd also inherited his mother's eyes, the color an unusual violet-blue. He blinked at the assembled group for a moment, taking it all in, before offering a huge grin, proudly displaying a pair of bottom teeth.

Kiley couldn't resist. It was a night of new experiences and fate offered her one more she wanted to add to her collection. "May I?" she asked. "I can't remember ever holding a baby before."

Rosalyn instantly melted. "Joshua's still half-asleep, so I'm not sure how he'll take to you. Just don't be offended if he decides he wants to go to Joc. He's more of a guy's guy than a momma's boy."

Kiley took the baby into her arms, cradling him in her arms, barely daring to breathe. Joshua blinked up at her and she could tell he was weighing his options—scream his little head off or put up with her. To her delight, he gave her the benefit of the doubt.

"He's almost a year, and yet he still smells so new," she whispered to Nicolò.

He chuckled, joining her on the couch and wrapping an arm around her and the baby. "Try smelling him when he loads that diaper of his."

"Amen," Joc and Rosalyn said in unison.

The rest of the evening passed, possessing an almost dreamlike quality. Contentment settled over Kiley, along with a renewed self-confidence. Maybe she could handle this, especially if all Nicolò's friends were as nice as the Arnauds. She continued to hold Joshua, who promptly fell asleep against her breast.

"Lucky brat," Nicolò whispered in her ear.

"No," she whispered back. "Lucky me."

When the evening came to an end, Kiley reluctantly handed over Joshua and she and Nicolò made their farewells. They followed the lighted walkway from the Arnauds' cabana to their own, enjoying the exotic scents that filled the sultry night air. It gave Kiley a moment to think, to address the whispered concerns that had gradually grown to a shout during the course of the evening. She'd learned two very important facts this evening.

First, that she could act the part Nicolò required of her in order to fit into his world. And second, she didn't want to pretend to be anyone other than herself, the *real* woman she instinctively recognized as her true persona. Now, she had to convince her husband of that. Nicolò unlocked the door and waited for her to precede him into the darkened interior. She paused in the foyer and turned to face him.

"I can't continue this pretense any longer," she announced.

Chapter Six

Nicolò froze, Kiley's words causing bitter disappointment to clash with cynical triumph. *Gotcha.* He didn't know what about tonight had set her off, but she was finally going to admit the truth of who and what she was.

"Then end the pretense and put your cards on the table," he challenged.

"Okay, fine." She swiveled to face him, taking a step in his direction that shifted her from deep shadow into a pool of moonlight. "I can't continue living this sort of lifestyle. It feels wrong. *I* feel wrong," she emphasized.

Okay, not quite what he expected. "You didn't enjoy this evening?"

"This evening—or at least, the second half of the evening—was incredible. But not all the rest. Not the trappings and the facade I'd have to adopt." Worry filled her expression. "Is it necessary, Nicolò? Do I have to become the woman I was before in order for our relationship to work?"

"No." The word escaped before he could stop it. "You can be any sort of woman you wish."

She caught her bottom lip between her teeth, apprehension filling her expression. She sawed at her lip for a telling moment before the words burst from her. "And you'll still love me?"

The question burned like acid. "My feelings for you won't change."

"Even though I've changed?"

"Give it time, sweetheart."

She took another step in his direction, closing the gap between them. Her hands slipped across his chest and she gathered up handfuls of his shirt. "I don't want to be the Kiley you described to me earlier. How can I like or respect her if she's as shallow inside as she is on the outside? I just want to be who I am now. Can you live with that? Can you accept that?"

He wasn't the one who wouldn't accept it. She, herself, wouldn't. Couldn't. Not once she regained her memory. But how did he explain that to her, without telling her the rest?

"It's not my decision," he said, regret roughening his voice. "If your memory returns you'll be who you were before. Any events that occur since then may alter your perspective, somewhat. But you'll be the Kiley O'Dell I first met."

Tears filled her eyes and she shook her head. "I can almost hear the clock ticking down. Only in this version I don't know who or what Cinderella turns into when the clock strikes midnight. I'm afraid of that other woman, afraid I'll turn into something or someone I won't like."

"I don't understand. Don't you want to remember?"

"Yes. No. The way you act—" She shook her head, her tears catching on the end of her lashes. "The way everyone acts makes me wonder what you're not telling me. Even Rosalyn—"

Aw, hell. "What about her?"

"She was annoyed with you about something. Please don't deny it," Kiley added, before he had a chance to speak. "All that business about being vulnerable and having to trust you. I can read between the lines. I also overheard you and Francesca arguing at Dantes Exclusive. I'm not an idiot, Nicolò. You're keeping something from me. What is it?"

"It's nothing."

The tears fell then, each one impacting like a knife to the gut. "You're lying," she whispered, not even attempting to disguise her pain. "You said we fought right before my accident. Were we about to break up? Is that it? Is that what you can't bring yourself to tell me? Are you just waiting until my memory returns before you put an end to our marriage?"

"We did argue," he admitted. "And it's possible that when your memory returns you'll want to end our relationship."

"Why?"

He shook his head. "Call it irreconcilable differences."

"What happens if I never regain my memory?" she persisted. "If I never remember, do we continue to pretend there isn't a problem? For how long?"

"You'll get it back." He said it with such flat certainty, she flinched.

"What if I don't?" The question sounded more like a wish and a prayer. "What happens then?"

"I don't have an answer for you."

"That's why you initially put me in a separate bedroom. Why we haven't made love. Why you're insisting I regain my memory before we do. Because we were on the verge of divorce."

"It was an argument, Kiley. That's all."

She took a step back, releasing him. Her eyes glittered like crystal in the moonlight, leached of all color. She reached for the first button of her blouse and thumbed it through the hole. Then a second. And a third. The deep V of her neckline revealed the intricate heart-shaped locket on its thin silver chain.

It was almost identical to their first meeting at Le Premier when she'd tempted him with that tantalizing striptease. Only this time around, he didn't catch a flash of vibrant red. This time he couldn't tell what color provided such a sharp contrast between the milky whiteness of her skin and the unrelenting darkness of her blouse. This time her movements stuttered with a hint of clumsiness and sweet resolve, rather than cynical calculation.

His gaze shot to her face and he searched for some hint to her thoughts, some clue that she was playing him by reenacting their initial meeting. But he saw nothing other than a fierce determination.

She finished unbuttoning her blouse and shrugged it off. It crumpled to the floor behind her. She kicked aside her sandals before tugging at the snap of her jeans. Next came the rending of her zipper, the sound shattering in the dense silence of the foyer. She slipped the denim off her narrow hips, her no-nonsense movements in complete opposition to her provocative actions during their hotel room meeting.

She stood before him in bra and panties. They were much plainer than before, and for some reason far more tantalizing. When he made no attempt to touch her, she reached behind her back and unfastened her bra and tossed it to one side. And then her panties disappeared as simply and economically as her jeans.

Moonlight poured over her, silvering the creamy white of her skin and creating interesting shadows beneath the slight curve of her breasts, as well as in the nest of curls at the junction of her thighs. It also spotlighted a small birthmark riding the curve of her hip, one that reminded him of a flower in full bloom.

Some might have called her figure boyish. Nicolò found it anything but. Her arms and legs were sculpted with lean muscle with just enough curves to make them distinctly feminine in appearance. Her breasts were on the small side, certainly, but they were also round and pert, with the nipples forming perfect pearls that he longed to taste. She was so delicate, her ankles and wrists coltish-slender. And yet, she was all woman, an indomitable woman at that, determined to tempt him beyond endurance.

The Inferno woke with a roar, consuming him in huge greedy gulps, filling him with an insatiable hunger. In that moment he didn't care who she'd been before. All that mattered was here and now. They belonged together and he refused to deny the fact any longer. He'd deal with the fallout from his actions when Kiley regained her memory. In the meantime, he'd take what she so generously offered. Take it and be damned grateful because when she came to her senses, she'd make him pay.

Big-time.

In one swift stride he reached her and swept her into his arms. "I hope you know what you're doing," he told her.

Her arms whipped around his neck and clung. "Not even a little. Not that I care."

"I'll remind you of that at some point down the road."

"I won't forget." Her expression grew fierce. "Not this time."

He shouldered his way into their bedroom and dropped her onto the mattress. She came up on her knees, lost amid the flow of creamy silk covering the mile-wide bed. He didn't waste any time. He stripped out of his clothes and joined her.

And then he paused. Slowed. Allowed himself to savor the moment.

The moonlight had followed them in here and caught in the long curls of her hair. He could just make out a whisper of blush in the pale color, as well as the merest hint of green in the eyes she trained so steadily on him. "The light?" he asked, remembering how she hated the dark.

"It's not necessary." She cupped his face and lifted upward, fitting her mouth to his. "Not any longer."

He sank into her, home at last. "Are you sure," he murmured between a series of long, drugging kisses.

"Positive."

"No regrets come morning?"

"No regrets, ever."

His smile held little humor. "Don't be so sure of that."

"And I'm guessing you aren't going to explain that particular remark, either."

"No." He lost his hands in the weight of her hair. "But there's one thing I want you to know and believe."

Her head tipped back giving him better access to the length of her neck. "And what's that?"

He slid his index finger along the pulse throbbing in her throat before following the same path with his tongue. "It was like this between us from the first moment we met. From the instant I set eyes on you, I wanted you."

"Was the feeling mutual?"

"You know the answer to that."

She smiled, the curve of her lips full of mystery and allure. "I responded the same way as I did at the hospital." It wasn't a question.

"Yes."

"I may have no memory," she whispered. "But I know you. I know your touch and your scent. I know the sound of your heartbeat and how it echoes my own. I know you were meant to be mine, just as I was meant to be yours."

He shook his head. "Kiley—"

She stopped his words with her hand. "I'm serious, Nicolò. On some level I must remember you. It's as if you imprinted yourself on my heart and soul. Can't we just start over, as though our fight never happened?"

He closed his eyes. "It won't change anything. Not in the long run. Not when you regain your memory."

She shifted, opening herself to him. "I'm willing to take the chance."

The last of his resistance vanished. He lowered himself to her, sliding over her. Skin burned against skin. Curves and angles collided before shaping themselves, one to the other. She was soft, so soft. It took every ounce of control to keep from burying himself in that softness. And then a stray thought took hold.

If her memory loss was real, if she couldn't remember anything of her life before, then she also didn't remember making love. For her this would be another new experience. And even if she regained her memory at some point, this night would, quite possibly, hold special meaning for her. How could he do anything other than make it as unique for her as possible?

He slowed the pace, taking her mouth in slow, deep kisses. And all the while he gave to her, gifted her with quiet caresses and teasing strokes. With whispered words that brought a flush of warmth to cheek and breast. He let her know with every touch, with every appreciative murmur, with every sweep of his hand that he found her the most beautiful woman he'd ever held in his arms. And she believed him, because it was the truth.

"Is this how it was the first time we were together?" she marveled at one point.

He couldn't lie. Not here. Not now. Not in such an intensely intimate moment when they were both stripped to their bare essence. "This isn't like any other time. This is new for both of us."

Her breath escaped in a happy sigh. "I'm glad. I want it to be different. I want it to be special."

And it would be. He'd see to that. He cupped her breasts, as tantalizing and perfect as the rest of her, and lathed the sensitive tips. She arched beneath him, pressing herself deeper into his mouth. He scraped the tight nipples with his teeth and heard the soft cry of pleasure it elicited. And then he tormented her other breast, feeling the pounding of her heart against his cheek.

The need to taste more of her drew him and he slid downward, sampling the soft indentation of her belly and the small birthmark at her hip, before finding the thick blush of curls concealing the heart of her. He parted the delicate folds and gave her the relief her body wept for. Her hips rose to meet his kiss, her thighs taut and trembling as she teetered on the knife's edge. He pushed, ever so slightly, and she went over with a cry, all fluid heat and gasping pleasure.

"We're not done, yet," he warned. "Not even close to done."

"I don't want this to ever end." Her hands curled in his hair and she tugged, drawing him up and over her. "I want this night to last forever."

She was so beautiful, still captured within the moon-silvered glow of her climax. "It's not within my power to make the night last forever." He traced her features, one by one. The winged arch of her brows, the wide, vivid eyes, her sculpted cheekbones and pert nose, right down to her sweetly lopsided smile. "But the memory of tonight will last forever."

Her smile faded. "What if I forget again?"

His gaze grew tender. "Then I'll remember for you."

Tears gathered in her eyes. "I'd like that."

He began again, building on what had gone before. Her reaction to him came quicker this time, her responses more natural and fluid. And she gave back in ways that threatened to send him straight out of his mind.

Her quick, clever hands stroked and gripped before flitting away to provoke a new sensation. And she moved—heaven help him, how she moved—with a sensual grace that drove him wild with desire. She flowed over his body like silk, cupping him, tracing a provocative finger of exploration across velvet and steel. By the time she finished she knew every inch of his body. But then, he knew every inch of hers.

Finally, the exploration ended in the ultimate discovery. Making short work of slipping on protection, he parted her thighs and forged deep inside. She wrapped herself around him, clinging to him as though she never intended to let go. And then she rocked upward, surging with him into a rhythm as old as mankind.

Nicolò could feel the white-hot forging of The Inferno, could feel the ultimate completion of the bond between them and the way it expanded until it filled him to overflowing. It didn't matter any longer whether Kiley was con artist or innocent. They belonged together, two parts of a whole. How their affair would ultimately end was a question for another time and place. All that mattered was here and now.

This moment.

This woman.

The creation of this memory, everlasting.

She shuddered beneath him. "No, not yet."

"Now, Kiley. Go over with me."

Their gazes locked, his demanding, hers so trusting it would haunt him forever. He cupped her head as he surged inward, watching her give in and take flight. Feeling her surrender radiate outward until it encompassed her entire body. And he soared with her, losing himself in her heat and warmth. Losing himself in that moment of ultimate completion. Losing himself, body and soul.

"How could I have forgotten that?" she whispered in the darkness. "How is it possible that something so—"

"Perfect?" The word escaped without thought.

"Yes. *Perfect.*" She didn't speak for a long moment, and then added, "I thought when we made love I'd remember. That the strength of it would bring the past back to me."

He couldn't help himself. He froze. "It didn't?"

Her breath escaped in a frustrated sigh. "No. I only have this one memory of us together. All the other times are—" Her hand fluttered through the air. "Gone."

Her voice broke on that last word and she curled into him, her tears biting into his skin. All he could do was hold her while she wept and allow the guilt to eat him alive. He couldn't doubt her any longer, at least not about her amnesia. Whatever she'd been before was currently trapped in the dark recesses of her mind, perhaps forever.

So where did the two of them go from here? He'd taken her on as his responsibility, claimed her as his own. Worse, he'd taken advantage of her vulnerability. If she'd been a scam artist, what did that make him?

He closed his eyes, flinching from the question. Up until now he could justify his actions. Could claim he was acting for the better good of his family. But what he'd done this night wasn't for anyone's benefit but his own. Hell, he could blame it on The Inferno, could claim their ending up in bed together was inevitable. But at least he knew all the facts, had taken this step with total awareness and understanding.

Kiley hadn't. Worse, she believed they were married, that when she'd given herself to him, it had been a wife to her husband. He pulled her close and kissed the top of her head. She murmured drowsily and snuggled closer. No question about what was going to happen as a result of his actions tonight, especially if his "wife" regained her memory anytime soon.

He was going straight to hell.

"What are you up to, Nicolò Dante?" Kiley faced her husband, her hands planted on her hips. Not that she appeared terribly intimidating, an impossible feat when dressed in a minuscule bikini, her modesty barely preserved by the paper thin floral *pareo* she'd wrapped around her hips. "You have secret written all over you."

"A small deviation in plans."

"We're not reenacting another date?" she asked, unable to prevent a small twinge of disappointment.

He shook his head. "Since you ended up in tears the one time we attempted it, I'd rather not. Instead, I decided to try something else. You gave me the idea last night when you were holding Joshua."

She stared blankly. "I did?"

"You did." He adjusted her hat to ensure her pale skin remained shaded from the powerful rays of the sun. "You commented that holding a baby was a new experience for you. So, I've decided to give you a few more new experiences. They're waiting for you on the beach."

He led her toward the lagoon outside their cabana and she paused halfway across the sand, staring in amazement. A huge table had been assembled beneath a canvas tent, the linen-covered surface overflowing with food, drinks, and even flowers.

"What's all this?" she asked in astonishment.

"These are new memories." He gestured toward the table. "We're starting with appetizers and ending with dessert. There's a little of everything."

It took her a moment to reply, a series of emotions sweeping across her face. Surprise.

Fascination. Curiosity. And sweet, utter delight. "And the flowers?"

"I had them gather up every variety they had in stock. You decide which ones you like best."

Her expression grew misty. "Oh, Nicolò, this is so thoughtful of you."

She threw her arms around him and lifted her mouth to his. He took his time with the kiss, sparking a return of the passion they'd shared the previous night. Before she could act on it, he caught her hand in his and drew her across the sand to the tent. Once inside, he considered the flowers and finally plucked one from the various arrangements, one she wouldn't have expected.

"Honeysuckle?" she asked. "Do I make you think of honeysuckle?"

He hesitated. "One of my earliest memories is wandering through my grandfather's garden. He has this beautiful pink honeysuckle growing along one of the fence lines. I couldn't have been much more than three, but that scent drew me. It was indescribable. I think I got drunk on the perfume."

She leaned in and inhaled the delicate sweetness. "It's wonderful."

"It was my first flower, or at least my first memory of one. My first floral scent."

"It's your favorite, isn't it? That's why you're sharing it with me."

"Yes. Though I learned to be cautious around a hedge of blooming honeysuckle."

"Uh-oh. Bees?" she hazarded a guess.

"'Fraid so. That day was also my first bee sting."

She frowned. "One of your favorite memories is also one of your most painful?"

He inclined his head. "I've discovered that's often the way life works."

"Why, Mr. Dante, you're a cynic."

"Comes with the territory, I'm afraid. As Dantes' troubleshooter I see all the problems. It's my job to fix them."

"Regardless of the cost?"

"Yes." He gave her a direct look, one that seemed to chill the humid warmth of the midday air. "And sometimes that cost is very high."

"You don't have to worry about that now," she told him, her tone taking on a fierce edge. "You don't have to troubleshoot a problem while we're on Deseos. Not here. Not with me. You can relax and enjoy yourself while we have fun playing."

Curls danced along her temples, tightened by the unrelenting humidity, and he tucked them behind her ear, anchoring them in place with the sprig of honeysuckle. "You, my dear, cause me nothing but trouble."

He said it with such a look of good humor she couldn't take offense. "Well, as long as I'm already trouble for you, why don't we see how much more I can cause you?" She shot him a flirtatious glance from beneath the brim of her hat. In response, heat flared to life in his dark eyes. "What do you say we dive into that table of new memories?"

The rest of the day was one of sheer delight and endless sensual pleasure. It wasn't just the food or flowers or drink, but who she shared them with. *Nicolò*. Nicolò, who left her in fits of laughter one minute and in the next moved her to tears with his poignant stories of family. Nicolò, who turned her life golden with a single smile. As the sun slipped away, and the shadows grew long, she went into his arms.

"Thank you for such an incredible day," she told him.

She lifted her mouth to his in order to sample the sweetest of all the desserts. This put the final touch on their time together. This made it perfect. His reaction to her was instantaneous. He tugged her close, wrapping his arms around her with a power and strength that reminded her of their night together. He'd put those skillful hands on her the previous evening, used that strength and power—and gentleness—to drive her insane with desire.

She caught his lower lip between her teeth and tugged. With a groan, he opened to her and she slid into rich, lush warmth. Drowned in it. Drowned in him. "Please, Nicolò," she whispered against his mouth. "After all the new, I need something old. Not too old," she hastened to add. "Just a little old. A slight bit repetitive."

"One night old?" he suggested with a soft chuckle.

"Yeah. That should do it."

Without a word, he turned her toward the cabana and they walked hand-in-hand into the dusky interior. One by one, clothes were discarded, creating a pathway of color from doorway to bedroom. There was a different quality to their lovemaking this time. Less desperation. No, she decided with a muffled groan. She still felt desperate, in the best possible way. But there was less uncertainty. She had a better idea what to do and how to do it. And she put that knowledge to work.

Where before he'd taken charge, had guided the pace and rhythm, this time she took the lead. With each stroking caress, her confidence grew, as did her creativity. And then intent dissolved in the face of helpless passion. There was no follower or leader, just the two of them, lost in one another, drowning in glorious sensation. Reveling in touch and possession.

She took him in, hard and deep, moved with him, seeking that moment, that sweet, sweet moment when the melding would come, when two were mated into one. At last it hit, an uncontrollable rolling that crashed over her and sent her up and over. And as she tumbled, helpless beneath the hugeness of it, she realized she'd just experienced something else new, new and infinitely precious.

She'd just discovered how to love.

Chapter Seven

Nicolò and Kiley ended up spending five more delicious days and nights on Deseos; bright, shiny moments she treasured and held close to her heart. Although their original plan had been to duplicate the dates they'd enjoyed leading up to their island marriage—dates she still couldn't recall—she much preferred Nicolò's change of plan. Instead of repeating the old, he'd filled their time together with an endless tumble of new sensations, memories she'd always treasure.

Finally, the time came for their return to San Francisco and she packed away the memories with as much care as their various purchases. On the return trip, she and Nicolò curled up together, laughing softly over various highlights of their trip while exchanging deep, leisurely kisses.

Once they landed, they grabbed a cab that let them off in front of Nicolò's house. He carried the luggage they'd acquired on Deseos onto the broad, wraparound porch and stacked them to one side of the door before turning to address Kiley.

"My grandparents dropped Brutus off first thing this morning, which means he's going to need a walk. He has a fenced run out back, but it doesn't give him the amount of exercise he requires." He shot her a warning look. "You might want to stand back. Chances are, he'll be a bit exuberant."

Kiley decided to opt for the smarter course and wait on the sidewalk while Nicolò dealt with the massive animal. The instant he inserted the key in the lock she could feel the initial rumblings of the earthquake signaling the dog's approach. To her amusement instead of greeting Nicolò with their usual bonding ritual, Brutus shot past him and headed straight for her. Between his massive jaws he carried a much-abused tennis ball.

Kiley greeted the dog with a thorough scratch behind his ears and picked up the ball he dropped at her feet. "You want to play catch?" she asked.

Brutus spun around, barking in excitement. To Kiley's horror, he bounded into the street. Behind her, Nicolò shouted in warning, a mirror to her own panicked cry. She saw the dog hesitate in confusion, then crouch down in his sphinxlike pose, holding perfectly still.

After that, events seemed to unravel in slow motion. Kiley swung her head to the left and saw a massive SUV heading for the motionless dog. Without a moment's hesitation, she charged toward the road, running on sheer instinct. Pelting toward Brutus, she grabbed for his collar. But even as she did so, she knew she'd reached him too late. She was nowhere near strong enough to drag the dog clear of danger before the SUV hit them.

She didn't see the vehicle's final approach, only heard the harsh blare of horn and the sickening squeal of brakes. She acted without thought, throwing herself across Brutus in a ridiculous attempt to protect him, not that she covered more than half the animal. Then she braced herself for the inevitable impact she knew would follow.

The horn and brakes continued their endless scream of warning and for a brief instant, something flashed through her mind. A memory. A memory that caused such pain and panic, every part of her cringed from it. In that split second of time she wasn't outside Nicolò's house, but found herself in the middle of a different street, where something bright yellow with blue fenders came barreling toward her. Before she could fully grasp the memory, it slipped away, along with all the foggy wisps of that other time and place, of that other Kiley.

The squeal of brakes seemed to last forever before the SUV slid to a stop mere inches from where Kiley had her head buried in Brutus's thick coat. The vehicle came so close she could feel the heat pouring off the engine hovering inches above her ear, and smell the distinctive oil and radiator stench that clogged her lungs and made it impossible to breath.

She vaguely heard the driver shout in a bizarre combination of anger and concern. Vaguely heard Nicolò's response before the driver took off with another punch of the car horn that left her trembling in reaction. Vaguely heard Brutus's whimper, as well as Nicolò's voice coming from somewhere above her.

She couldn't move. Couldn't process thought or any of the reassurances Nicolò offered in his soft, gentle rumble of a voice. She didn't even think she could feel, until Brutus washed the tears from her face and Nicolò lifted her from her prone position. Then she felt far, far too much. With a wordless cry, she dissolved against her husband, sobbing uncontrollably.

"Easy, sweetheart. You're okay. You're fine now."

"Bru-Brutus?" Her teeth were chattering so hard she could barely get the word out.

"He's fine." A snap of his fingers had the dog scurrying onto the porch, his tail between his legs. Nicolò followed, carrying her as though she were made of the most fragile porcelain. "What the hell were you thinking, running into the street after him like that?" He sounded angry, but even in her current state she understood the anger came from fear.

She sagged against him. "Wasn't thinking. Not even a little. I just . . ." The chatter of teeth hiccupped through her words. ". . . just reacted."

"That's obvious. Did you really believe you could protect Brutus by throwing yourself between him and a two-and-a-half ton SUV?"

She forced out a watery grin. "Haven't you figured it out, yet? I'm indestructible."

"Don't joke," he said, his voice tight and ragged. "You could have been killed. Again."

"But I wasn't. Again."

She pressed her mouth to his neck, inhaling the crisp, masculine scent of him. It stirred the oddest sensation, making her dizzy with need. How was that possible after what she'd just been through?

Nicolò put Kiley down long enough to toss their bags through the door before slamming it closed behind them. Then he picked her up again, intent on taking her to the bedroom. He managed a single step before sagging onto the floor in a jumble of arms, legs, luggage, and dog.

"Aw, hell." He wrapped her up tight. Too tight. But he couldn't seem to control his response. *"Damn it,* Kiley. I thought I'd lost you."

"I'm sorry." Her words tumbled out, nearly incoherent. "I just reacted. All I could think about was saving Brutus. I'm fine. We're both fine now."

"That's twice." He lowered his head and inhaled her, her scent, her touch, her taste. He snatched a half-dozen urgent kisses. "Twice I've watched you come within an inch of dying. And both times I wasn't able to get to you before—"

"I'm okay. I'm safe." She caught hold of Brutus's collar and tugged the dog into their circle. "And so is Brutus."

It was time to face facts, he realized. He didn't know the woman he'd met that day at Le Premier. Whoever she was, she bore no relationship to the Kiley he held in his arms. That woman, the one prior to the accident, wouldn't have risked her perfectly manicured pinky to save his dog. That woman wouldn't have relished the scent of a simple sprig of honeysuckle, or reveled in the experience of holding a sleeping baby in her arms. That version of Kiley was gone, with luck forever, and he could only thank God for it.

"Brutus, backyard," he ordered. As much as he adored his dog, right now he needed his wife.

No. Not his wife.

Not yet.

He cupped her face and covered her mouth in another kiss, only this one held a far different quality. Where before he'd been reassuring himself he'd reached her in time and she hadn't been harmed, this kiss was life-affirming. Fate had been kind to them both, had protected her not once, but twice. He'd see to it there wasn't a third incident. No matter what it took, he'd protect her from her own impulsiveness.

At the touch of his mouth, she opened to him, welcomed him home. Gave to him. He could feel his self-control slip as he lost himself in his desperate need for her.

"Now. I want you right here and right now."

She eased back and he snatched her into his arms again, unwilling to release her. "Wait," she said. Her laugh bubbled with happiness and desire and the sheer exhilaration of life. "I'm not going anywhere. You can have me wherever. Whenever. However."

"Here. Now. Naked."

Her laughter faded while her eyes heated. "In that case . . ."

Again she eased back and this time he let her go. Gripping the bottom of her shirt, she yanked it over her head and off. He didn't wait for her to remove her bra. His patience only stretched so far. No more than a few short seconds. With a flick of his fingers, he had the scrap of silk and lace open and swept aside.

She settled back onto his lap, back where she belonged, her legs cinching his waist. She started on the buttons of his shirt, but he didn't have the patience for that, either. In one button-spewing move, he shredded his shirt from stem to stern. Anything, if it meant having those clever hands of hers on his skin.

Heaven help him, but she was beautiful. Soft and tender and utterly edible. He cupped her bottom, gathered the slight weight of her in his palms. She tilted her head back with a groan, giving him total access to the elegant length of her throat and curve of her shoulders, long silken sweeps of skin that begged to be tasted and caressed. He gave her his full attention, finding every sensitive hollow and curve. And still it wasn't enough.

He tore at the snap and zip to her jeans, dragging them down her hips to reveal the flower-shaped birthmark stamped there, before peeling them off the pert curve of her backside. She wriggled clear of his lap just long enough for him to strip her. When he finished, she lay panting on the parquet floor, her skin sun-kissed gold against the dark wood, her hair full of red-hot flames. He ripped open his own jeans and took her hard and fast, sinking deep inside her in one powerful thrust while her cry of ecstasy echoed through the foyer.

He'd almost lost her. He might never have been able to hold her again. Kiss her. Make love to her. The mere thought left him crazed, gripped by a frenzy unlike anything he'd ever experienced before. He'd never been this desperate to have a woman. Never been so insane with desire that he hadn't cared about the where and when.

Until Kiley.

"Don't stop," she ordered. She clung to him, arms and legs wrapped tight around him, pulling him in until they were one flesh moving in unison. "Don't ever let go of me."

"Never. I swear I'm going to lock you away where no one can ever hurt you again."

She opened her mouth to reply, but instead arched upward, a keening cry ripped from her throat. She surrendered utterly to his possession, giving everything she had and holding nothing back. No hesitation, no subterfuge. Every stray thought and feeling there for him to see, his to accept or reject, more open and honest and giving than he believed it possible for a woman to be.

Her eyes turned a blinding shade of green, burning with an emotion so powerful and all-consuming it hurt to look at her. As he took her, as he sent her slamming into an endless climax, he realized it was love he saw in her eyes. A soul-deep commitment. And with that knowledge he went over the edge with her, lost to a moment that never should have happened.

It was a long time before he could move again. When he did, he realized nothing had changed. He had committed a crime beyond redemption and Kiley— He closed his eyes, utterly destroyed. Kiley had fallen in love with him. Gently, he lifted her in his arms and carried her to their bedroom. And all the while, two questions tormented him.

What the hell had he done?

And how could he fix it?

Kiley awoke the next morning, deliciously sore, yet thoroughly refreshed. On the pillow beside her, she found a businesslike note from Nicolò warning he'd be at the office all day. Beneath the first note she found a second, and there was nothing businesslike at all about this one. The few short sentences left her in no doubt of Nicolò's feelings about the night before and caused a blush of delight to warm her cheeks.

She grinned like a loon over the second note, while fighting a wave of disappointment over the first. Well, what did she expect? Because of her accident, he'd been forced to take countless days off. He must have mountains of work piled up as a result.

Bouncing out of bed, she spent the morning on domestic chores, unpacking their bags and washing clothes. As the clock edged toward noon, she decided to surprise her husband for lunch. During their time together she'd gotten a fair idea of his tastes, and made up her mind to create a silly meal loaded with his favorites, everything from chicken Marsala to *panzanella*, pistachios to bitter chocolate, all easily available with just a few quick phone calls.

The instant the various treats arrived, she loaded them into a basket she found in a cupboard above the refrigerator and decorated it with a sprig of honeysuckle she found growing along the backyard fence. She liked to think Nicolò had started the hedge from a cutting he'd taken from his grandfather's garden, a tribute to that long-ago encounter with his first flower, not to mention his first bee sting.

Next, she called for a cab, relieved to discover the driver knew just where to find Dantes' corporate headquarters. The cabbie dropped her off in front of an impressively large office building and she entered through the revolving doors. Once inside she stumbled to a halt, staring in awe at the spectacular three-story glass foyer. She took her time, admiring everything from the elegant decor to the dance of sunlight off the sheets of tinted windows, to the impressive glass sculpture of dancing flames that hung above the receptionist's desk.

She'd just started toward the desk when an elderly man with a thick thatch of snowy hair approached. "Please, excuse me," he said, his deep voice carrying the lilting cadence of a Mediterranean heritage. "Are you Kiley O'Dell?"

She smiled warmly. "Actually, it's Kiley Dante."

"Yes, of course." He gazed at her with assessing gold eyes, eyes that cut straight through all pretense and yet held an unmistakable glint of kindness. "I believe, my dear, it is past time we met. I am Primo Dante."

Her smile grew and she regarded him in genuine delight. "You're Nicolò's grandfather. He told me all about you and how you helped raise him and his brothers."

"Nicolò, Severo, and the twins. Yes, Nonna and I took them in after the death of our son, Dominic, and his wife, Laura." He took her hand in his and leaned in to kiss first one of her cheeks, then the other. "You are on your way to visit Nicolò?"

She indicated the basket she carried. "I thought he'd enjoy some lunch."

Primo's gnarled fingers brushed the honeysuckle blossom decorating the handle. "And what have you brought him?" He listened intently while she listed the eclectic jumble of flavors. She petered out uncertainly and he gave her a reassuring smile. "It would seem you know my grandson's tastes quite well. And for yourself? Have you put nothing of your own in here? Or is all this for Nicolò's benefit alone?"

She looked momentarily abashed. "Tapioca pudding," she admitted. She couldn't help laughing at herself. "Who'd have figured I'd develop such a taste for it?"

He chuckled. "You may find it interesting to discover what things appeal when you permit yourself to give them a try without a history to influence your choices."

"Or what things no longer appeal?" she asked.

His gaze grew even more shrewd. "Excellent observation." He gestured toward the bank of elevators toward the rear of the foyer. "Shall I escort you?"

"Thank you. I'd appreciate that."

Primo used a key to access a private car. "You are recovered from your accident?" he asked politely.

"Physically, yes." A slight frown tugged at her brow as they entered the elevator. "I still haven't regained my memory. Although . . ."

"Although?"

She hesitated, for some reason tempted to confess something to Primo that she hadn't even told her husband. "I might have remembered something yesterday." She detailed her near-miss from the day before. "Right before I thought the SUV would hit us, I had a flash of memory."

"And what was this flash?"

"I suspect it was from that first accident."

Primo gave a slow nod. "That would make sense. The similarity between the two incidents might prompt a return of your memory."

She turned to face him, staring up at a compassionate face lined with a wealth of experience, both good and ill. "And yet, my memory didn't come back, even though for a split second I recalled . . . something. Pain. Fear. And . . ."

"And?" he prompted. "What are you afraid to see, Kiley O'Dell?"

"Dante," she corrected. "I know I wasn't certain I wanted to take the name when Nicolò and I first married, but I think it's probably like tapioca pudding. Things that might not have been to my taste before, are now."

"You are avoiding my question."

She grinned. "You're right, I am." Her smile faded. "I was afraid of whatever I saw. I guess of the accident, of the pain it caused me."

"Or maybe you were afraid of that other life. Maybe when you had the choice to remember or forget, you chose to forget."

His words caused her heart to kick up a beat, possibly because they held the weight of truth. She caught her bottom lip between her teeth and worried at it. "You think I don't want to remember?" she finally asked.

Primo shrugged. "The mind is a strange thing. Perhaps it is protecting you. Perhaps when you no longer need its protection, you will remember." Before she could reply, the door slid open and he gestured for her to precede him. "You will find Nicolò's office at the end of the corridor to the left. Tell him it is time for you to meet the family. Tell him it is past time, yes?"

"Yes, it is," she agreed.

He leaned down and kissed her cheeks again, then headed in the opposite direction. Taking a deep breath, she followed Primo's directions, pausing outside a door with Nicolò's name on it. Some jokester had added a shiny gold label beneath his name that read Chief

Troublemaker. Her lips twitched and she lifted her fist to knock, hesitating at the last instant.

Was it possible? she couldn't help but wonder. Was she resisting remembering because she wanted to escape those memories? Could it all be tied in with the fight she'd had with Nicolò? Maybe if he told her what had happened it would cause her memory to return. Because despite how their marriage had functioned before her accident, they'd fully bonded since. And that meant they could find a way to work through whatever had divided them. She was convinced of it.

No matter what secret Nicolò kept from her, one thing was certain. The time had come for the two of them to be totally honest with one another, regardless of how painful the process. That decided, she rapped on the door, then turned the knob and walked in.

To her dismay, she found the room crowded with people. Three men stood in a pile, arguing at full throttle. None were Nicolò, though based on the fact that the three shared a physical similarity to her husband, and two of them were twins, they had to be his brothers. Off to one side sat a man with salt-and-pepper hair and a flushed complexion who silently seethed while he listened to the argument. He was flanked by yet another man, a huge tank-sized black man with black eyes that had been there and seen it all.

Finally, she located her husband, leaning against his desk, a grim expression darkening his face. At her entrance, his head jerked in her direction, and if anything, his expression turned blacker still.

He slowly straightened. "What are you doing here, Kiley?" he demanded in an undertone.

The salt-and-pepper-haired man glanced her way and leapt to his feet, pointing an accusing finger straight at her. "That's her! My God, you found the little bitch." He lunged toward her, his forward momentum stopped by the quick action of the three men Kiley had pegged as Nicolò's brothers. "Get out of my way," he roared. "I've waited a long time for this. Just give me five minutes of uninterrupted time alone with her and you can keep the money she owes me."

Kiley stumbled backward, relieved to find Nicolò planted in front of her, his stance clearly protective. "You shouldn't be here." He threw the comment over his shoulder. "Why did you come?"

"I—I brought you lunch. I wanted to surprise you." She swallowed, struggling to control the fear and tension tearing at her. "Surprise."

"Your timing couldn't have been worse."

"Who is that man? How does he know me? Why is he so angry?"

"The man is Jack Ferrell and he's leveled some accusations against you. The three by my desk are my brothers," he confirmed her guess by indicating the trio of men who'd been arguing when she'd first entered. "And Juice is Dantes head of security. We were trying to get to the bottom of the allegations when you arrived."

She stepped out from behind her husband, determined to face the accusations aimed at her head-on. The Dantes and Juice continued to restrain Ferrell while he ranted in undisguised fury. "What does he say I've done?"

Nicolò hesitated, then reluctantly explained, "He's accused you of scamming him out of a rather substantial sum of money."

"No." She shook her head. "That's not possible. I may not remember the past, but I do know myself. I wouldn't do anything so dishonest."

He turned to face her. "Kiley—"

"Oh, God." The lunch basket slipped from her fingers and hit the carpet, spilling its contents. The can of pistachios landed square on the honeysuckle, crushing the fragile blossoms. The sweet scent drifted up between them, sharp as a bee sting. "You believe him, don't you? You believe I ripped him off!"

Chapter Eight

To Kiley's horror, Nicolò didn't deny the accusation.

"Ferrell has proof, sweetheart," he said gently. "Granted, it's a bit on the sketchy side, but he insists you ran a con on him involving a fire diamond necklace, one you supposedly inherited from your grandfather."

"Fire diamonds?" For a split second she saw Francesca and Nicolò staring intently at her as she studied the fire diamonds at Dantes Exclusive, waiting . . . Waiting for what? For her to remember something about this necklace Ferrell referred to? Had they known about the accusations even then? "I don't understand any of this. What necklace does he mean?"

"I don't know. It's something we'll have to figure out together." She closed her eyes at his use of the word *together*. He must have understood how much it meant to her, because he traced his thumb along the curve of her cheek. "Until then, you need to go home."

"She's not going anywhere," Jack Ferrell protested. "I want my money. And I want her to pay for what she did to me. I insist you call the police and have her arrested."

Nicolò spun to face the man. "You signed a binding agreement, Ferrell. One that allows us to settle this matter quietly. It also requires you prove your claims. So far, all we have are accusations."

"She offered to sell me her grandfather's necklace. I put half the money down. But when I went to complete the transaction, she'd disappeared, along with my money and the necklace." He glared at Kiley. "You were slick, I'll give you that. But you won't get away this time."

Kiley shook her head, attempting to reason with the man. "I wouldn't do something like that. You must have me mixed up with someone else."

His lips pulled back in a snarl. "Not a chance in hell. You have a birthmark on your hip. It's shaped like a flower."

She felt every scrap of color drain from her face. Wordlessly, she shook her head.

"No? Come on, gorgeous. Strip down and show us the birthmark. Prove me wrong."

"Get out of here, Kiley," Nicolò interrupted. "I'll be home as soon as I resolve this."

"No. I'm not going anywhere. Not until the two of us discuss this." She spared a brief glance toward the other men. "Privately."

"Think you can sweet-talk your way around him?" Ferrell interrupted. "You're wasting your time. He's not the fool I was. With all the information his head of security has assembled, I'll bet he sees right through you. No way are you slipping out from under this one. Not this time."

Nicolò spun to face his brothers. "Shut him up, will you? I'll be right back." Without another word, he cupped Kiley's elbow and drew her from the room. "I can spare five minutes. We'll hash out the rest of it when I get home."

One look at his expression and everything went numb inside. This man wasn't her husband, wasn't the man who'd taken her with such crazed desperation on his foyer floor. This was the suspicious-eyed man from those first hours and days after her accident. Dear God. What had she done in that other life? What had she been?

She flinched from the possibility. Or maybe it was all some sort of colossal mistake. She'd never deliberately scam someone, would she? It didn't matter that Jack Ferrell knew about her birthmark. He could have found out about it somehow.

Kiley wrung her hands. If only she had her memory back, she could prove her innocence.

Without it, she was utterly vulnerable. She spared the grim stranger at her side a quick glance, unremitting pain lancing through her.

And utterly alone.

She remained silent and heartsick while Nicolò ushered her into a small conference room. Like everything else she'd seen of Dantes so far, it was a lovely room, but one clearly designed for business. Is that what she'd become? Business? Based on his current attitude, she might as well be.

She fought to gather her self-control, to focus her confusion into some semblance of order, so that at least she'd know what questions to ask. She opened with the first one to come to mind.

"Why did you Dantes' head of security look into me?"

"I asked Juice to check into some things after your accident."

"That doesn't quite answer my question," she pointed out. "But let's start there. Did you make the request because of my accident or because of our fight?"

"Does it matter?"

"Is what that man was saying—" She gestured in the general direction of Nicolò's office. "The necklace and the money I supposedly took from him. Is that what our fight was about? The one before my accident?"

"Indirectly."

Anger ripped through her. "Stop it, Nicolò. Just stop all the cagey responses and give it to me straight. I'll believe whatever you tell me." She laughed, a hard, painful sound. "After all, I don't have any other choice. Since I don't remember, I have to accept your version of events."

"The truth?"

"If you don't mind."

"Your grandfather and your great-uncle jointly owned a fire diamond mine, a mine they sold to my grandfather, Primo. When we first met it was to discuss the legality of that sale. You claimed there was a problem with the transfer of title, that you still owned a portion of the mine."

She took a moment to absorb that. "Then, we didn't meet over a game of Frisbee?"

"No."

She shook her head in bewilderment. "Why would you make up a story? What difference does it make how or when we met?"

"It mattered."

Frustration ripped through her. "Why?"

He rubbed a spot between his brows where tension had formed a deep crease. "I didn't want to bring it up after your accident because I needed time to find out whether your claim on the mine was genuine. I needed time for Juice to unearth the truth while you recovered from your injuries. Time for us to get to know one another, to deal with The Inferno, without the mine coming between us."

She frowned in confusion. "I still don't understand. What has the sale of the mine got to do with this necklace Ferrell is going on about?"

"I have no idea. If there's a connection, I haven't found it, yet. Juice met Ferrell while investigating you and your claims regarding the mine."

"This man, Ferrell, he's convinced I've scammed him, isn't he?"

"Yes."

"And you? What do you believe?"

"We're still looking into it, Kiley," he said with a painful lack of intonation. All the while, a remote darkness swirled in his gaze.

She could feel her heart breaking at the distance he put between them. Despite that, she forced herself to ask the necessary questions. "But it's possible he's right?" She could see the answer in Nicolò's expression and something infinitely precious died inside. It took a moment before she could form her next question, one almost too painful to ask. "Do you believe I was trying to scam you about the diamond mine?"

"Don't do this, Kiley. Not now."

"Answer me, Nicolò. When we first met, did you think I was some sort of con artist?"

He hesitated, before reluctantly nodding. "I suspected you might be."

"Why?" It was a cry from the heart.

He lifted his shoulder in a shrug, his expression one of extreme weariness. "Nothing definitive. Just a feeling I had."

She wanted to go to him, to wrap her arms around him and reassure him that it would all work out. But she couldn't. Too much divided them right now, a chasm of doubt and suspicion she had no clue how to bridge. Had no way of bridging without her memory.

"If you suspected me of being that sort of person, why did you decide to date me? How did we end up falling in love? How did we end up married?"

He lifted his hand, palm out. "It would seem The Inferno doesn't worry about such minor details as—"

"As moral character?" she cut in.

"Kiley—"

She glanced toward the door, realizing she was poised to run, to escape an untenable situation. The urge nearly overwhelmed her. Was it gut instinct, or a pattern so much a part of her it didn't require memory? She fought it with every ounce of strength she possessed. "Is it true? What Ferrell accused me of? Did I do those things? Is that who I really am?"

"I don't know." She could hear the frustration ripping apart his words. "I don't want to believe it, Kiley."

"Then don't." She dared to approach, dared to splay her hands across his chest and gather that steady, life-affirming heartbeat in her palm. "I need you to believe in me, Nicolò. I need you to fight for me. Maybe everything Ferrell says is true. Maybe I am a horrible person."

"No." The word escaped without thought or hesitation and it gave her the first glimmer of hope.

"Okay, *was*. Maybe I *was* a horrible person. But what if it's all a mistake? Since I can't remember, I can't defend myself. I have to believe there's some other explanation, if we can only find it." She stared up at him, no longer interested in running, but determined to fight. "Please, Nicolò. I need to discover the truth."

"And if the truth isn't what you want to hear?"

"At least it'll be the truth."

She shouldn't kiss him, shouldn't put any more pressure on him. But she couldn't help herself. Just for a moment or two she needed her husband, needed to coax him out from under his troubleshooter persona.

She slid her arms around his neck and covered his mouth with hers, practically consuming him. She felt his momentary resistance, understood it even as it caused her unfathomable pain. And then she felt the give, the gentle slide from reluctance into acceptance, before it transformed into something desperate and greedy and urgent. The flutter of hope gained in strength. He hadn't given up on her. Not yet.

She snatched another kiss, a final one. "I need you to promise me something else," she said.

She could see the shutters slam back into place. "If I can."

"Promise me you'll tell me the truth from now on. When you're done here, we'll put all the cards on the table."

He gave a brief nod. "That's one promise I can make. Until then, go home and I'll join you there as soon as I'm able."

His eyes were dark with pain and haunted by secrets. He lowered his head and kissed her again. There was an unmistakable finality in the way he embraced her, as though acknowledging on some level that their relationship would never be the same again. This time when he released her, he took a step backward, distancing himself physically, as well as emotionally.

"Fair warning, Kiley. You won't like some of those cards I'm going to show you. They may very well end things between us."

There was nothing she could say to that, no way to reassure him or calm her own fears. He opened the conference room door for her and she sleepwalked through it. She headed for the elevators, but found herself continuing past them, unable to convince herself to leave. She never knew how long she wandered the corridors before Primo found her and gathered her up.

Murmuring in soothing Italian, he escorted her to a generous-sized office. He installed her in a large, deep-cushioned chair before crossing to a wet bar. Pouring her a drink, he handed it to her. She cupped her hands around the balloon of the snifter and inhaled the potent brandy before taking a generous swallow.

Primo didn't say anything to her, but resumed his seat at his desk and occupied himself with paperwork. She sat and sipped the brandy, losing track of time. It could have been minutes or hours. Time flowed in a confusing haze. But at long last she looked up.

"Lunch didn't go well," she announced in a low voice.

Primo set aside his papers and capped his pen. "I assumed as much."

"It's funny. For the past few weeks I've been enjoying so many new experiences. Until today. Today," She drew and deep breath and pushed out an unsteady smile. "Not so much."

"Sometimes we learn more from the bad experiences than the good."

She curled deeper in the chair. "I'm not sure I like that idea."

He cocked a head to one side in a gesture endearingly reminiscent of Nicolò. "Perhaps you have learned what you now must fix. Would that not allow some good to come from the bad?"

"I can fix being a con artist?"

His gaze sharpened. "So. You believe this man, Ferrell."

It shouldn't surprise her he'd heard about what had happened in Nicolò's office. The Dantes were a tight-knit family. "Ferrell knows things about me. Things he shouldn't—" Her voice broke and she struggled to control it. She met his golden gaze, caught the compassion gleaming there and allowed it to warm her.

"What if he's right? What if I really am a scam artist?"

"Are you?" He paused a beat. "Or *were* you?"

Tears filled her eyes. "Is there a difference?"

"Very much so. One exists in a past you cannot recall. The other may be created in a future yet to come."

His words struck hard, restored the hope that had been so badly shaken. "Thank you, Primo." She uncurled from her chair and crossed the room to plant a kiss on his cheek. "I'm glad we finally met."

He stood and enfolded her in a tight embrace. "As am I."

Nicolò had told her to go home, but she couldn't bear the idea of returning there without him. Instead, she retraced her path to his office, hoping he'd now be available to leave with her. To her disappointment, the door stood open and the room deserted. She entered, intent on scribbling him a brief note. Crossing to his desk, she saw a folder bearing her name on the wooden surface. Curiosity got the better of her and she flipped it open.

And her world collapsed around her.

Nicolò had to be home, waiting for her, Kiley decided as she left Dantes. And when she arrived, she'd have him explain all she'd found in that damning file, a file currently tucked beneath her arm. There had to be an explanation, other than the obvious one. She couldn't be the person detailed between those pages. It wasn't possible.

To Kiley's disappointment, she arrived to find an empty house, empty except for Brutus, who seemed to sense her despair. He trailed behind her, whining softly, as she wandered from room to room, struggling to come to terms with all she'd learned. From deep within the house, she heard the doorbell ring and for a split second her heart leaped. *Nicolò*. He was home. Then common sense prevailed. Her husband would have used his key.

Leaving Brutus in the den, she crossed to the front door and opened it, surprised to discover a woman standing there, impatiently tapping her foot.

"About time," the woman announced, before sweeping inside. "Do you have any idea how long it's taken me to track you down? I finally tricked your address out of the hospital, though what the hell you were doing there, they wouldn't say."

"Who—" Kiley hesitated, taking a second, longer look.

The woman, a striking blonde, appeared to be in her late thirties, though something about the hardness around her carefully made up eyes and mouth hinted at a handful of years more than that. She matched Kiley's stature, or lack thereof, the only difference between them the extra few inches the older woman carried in the bust line and around the hips. She wore her hair in a short cap of curls that emphasized both her striking bone structure, as well as a pair of vivid blue eyes.

A possibility occurred to Kiley, one she could only pray was true. "I know this is going to sound like an odd question, but . . . Are you my mother?" she asked, fighting to control a wild surge of emotion.

A single eyebrow winged skyward. "Have you lost your mind? Of course, I'm your mother."

"Oh, my God." Kiley threw her arms around the woman, hugging her with tearful exuberance. She needed this, needed something to go right today. "Oh, Mom, you have no idea how happy I am to meet you."

"Now I know you've lost your mind." The woman pried herself free of Kiley's embrace. "What the hell do you mean you're happy to meet me? And—horror of horrors—since when have you called me 'Mom'? Try Lacey, you ungrateful brat. Now where's the damn necklace?"

Kiley fell back a step. "I—I call you Lacey?"

"If you don't pull yourself together, I swear I'm going to slap you, if only to knock an ounce of sense into that brain of yours. I mean, really, Kiley. What were you thinking? What made you believe for one tiny second that you could get away with it?"

"Get away with—" She shook her head. "You don't understand. I was in an accident. I lost my memory. I have no idea what you're talking about."

To Kiley's shock, Lacey burst out laughing. "Oh, that's a good one. You're always scheming, aren't you? Well? Come on." She folded her arms across her chest and set her foot to tapping again. "Explain how this latest one works. I'm all ears."

Kiley stared at her mother in horror. Didn't she believe her own daughter? But then, if the information in the file was correct, why would she? "You don't understand. I'm serious. I have no memory of you, or of my past, or—or anything."

"Oh, you poor dear." Lacey feigned a sympathetic look before spoiling it with a laugh. "I have to hand it to you, sweetie, you're really quite good at this. I'm actually starting to enjoy myself, which is rather miraculous considering my mood when I arrived." She crossed to Kiley's side and linked arms with her. "Now don't keep your dear momma standing in the hallway. Show me around the joint."

Every instinct Kiley possessed screamed a warning. "Why don't we go into the living room," she suggested instead. "Maybe I can give you a tour when Nicolò gets home. He's due any moment."

"Nicolò?"

"My husband."

Lacey's jaw dropped. "You're married?"

"Close to a month now." She gestured toward the sofa. "Can I fix you a drink?"

"The usual. Make it a double."

"And the usual is?"

Lacey shrugged. "I should have known you'd be too good to fall for that one. Double scotch. Neat." She waited until she'd been served before leaning forward with a wheedling expression. "Come on, Kiley. Let me in on this one. I can play it anyway you want. Just give me the lowdown so I don't make any mistakes."

Kiley stared at her mother in disbelief. Oh, God. If this was the lifestyle she'd chosen before being hit by that cab, no wonder she didn't want to remember. How had she lived with herself?

How had she justified such an unscrupulous existence? "This isn't a scam. I was hit by a cab and I'm suffering from something called retrograde amnesia."

Lacey waved that aside. "Whatever. At least tell me who your mark is."

Mark. With every word her mother uttered, she confirmed the information in the file—hideous, damning information that listed name after name, amount after amount, of people scammed and money taken. "There is no mark," Kiley stated numbly. "There's just my husband."

Lacey snapped her fingers. "Right. The husband. That's one I haven't pulled in a while. Too messy." She gestured for Kiley to continue. "Well? What's his name?"

"Nicolò Dante."

"Dante?" Lacey sat bolt upright. *"Nicolò Dante?* Have you lost your mind? You think you can take down a Dante?"

"I keep telling you," Kiley said wearily. "This isn't—"

"A scam. Right." Lacey slammed her drink onto the coffee table with such force it made the crystal sing and gathered up her purse. "Well, I don't want any part of whatever it isn't."

"Just answer a question first." Kiley crossed to where she'd left the file. Flipping it open, she removed one of the pages and offered it to Lacey. "Do you recognize these names? Is this information correct? Did I rip off all these people?"

With notable reluctance, Lacey set aside her purse and took the paper. Scanning it, she turned deathly pale as she read. "What the hell are you thinking, writing all this down?" she gritted out. "Do you have any idea what sort of trouble this could cause us?"

"All I want to know is whether or not it's accurate. Did I do those things?"

Lacey shot to her feet, shoving the list back into Kiley's hands. "That's it. I don't know what you're trying to pull, but I won't be party to it. I suggest you burn that paper before someone connects you with it. In the meantime, I'm out of here." She held out her hand. "Just give me the necklace and I'll be on my way."

Kiley stiffened. There it was again. The necklace. No doubt the same necklace Ferrell referred to. She carefully folded the list into fours and slipped it into her pocket. "What necklace?"

"Stop playing games." Lacey's voice could have cut glass. "Your grandfather Cameron's fire diamond necklace."

Kiley stilled. "Then, there really is a necklace?"

"Of course there really is a necklace. Now where is it?"

"I haven't got a clue." Kiley began to laugh. "Maybe when I get my memory back, I'll remember that, as well."

"The locket." Lacey's anger ebbed, replaced by a look of cunning. "If you don't have the necklace on you, you've got a safe deposit key hidden in the locket."

Kiley slipped her hand beneath her blouse and fisted her fingers protectively around the silver heart. "So, I'm not just a scam artist. I get top marks for deviousness, too. Lovely."

She remembered with painful amusement how crushed she'd been when Nicolò had informed her she didn't have a close relationship with her mother. How she'd longed for the sort of family ties the Dantes possessed. Right now, she'd have given almost anything to be an orphan.

Kiley fished the locket from beneath her blouse. "FYI, I don't know how to open it."

"Oh, would you please give this amnesia business a rest? You had me in stitches with it earlier, but enough's enough." She took another step in Kiley's direction, her face lined with grim intent. "Give me the locket. I'll open it if you won't."

Her hand fisted around the locket. "I'm not giving you anything."

"You are such a fool," she ranted. "Do you think I didn't consider setting up the Dantes years ago? Color me with a bit more common sense than you're currently showing. At least I knew better than to make a play in that direction, though I will admit the amnesia thing gives it an interesting twist."

"It's not—"

"I'm your mother, Kiley," Lacey bit out. "You can't fool me. Now, I want that key. Give it to me or I swear I'll take it from you. I'm not playing around here. I don't want to be anywhere in the vicinity when Dante discovers you're faking amnesia in order to scam him."

"To late, I'm afraid." Nicolò stepped into the room, Brutus at his heels. "It would seem that Dante found out a little sooner than you anticipated."

Chapter Nine

It took every ounce of self-control for Nicolò to hold his fury in check. At his appearance, Kiley and her mother both spun to face him, identical expressions of consternation on faces that bore a startling similarity. Or they would if Kiley ever acquired the bitter cunning that marked the older woman's features.

Here was the avarice he'd sought in Kiley's face during their visit to Dantes Exclusive. The slyness. The self-indulgence. Finally, he could see what she worked so hard to keep from him. He only had to meet the mother to uncover it. Beside him, Brutus checked out the newcomer and released a soft growl, one that had her taking a hasty step backward.

"You asked for the truth, Kiley." He stripped off his suit jacket and tossed it over a nearby chair. "I didn't realize you were the one who would provide it for me."

"No, Nicolò." Her cheeks turned every bit as waxen as they'd been during her hospital stay, a realization that gave him an unwanted pang of concern. "You misunderstood what we were saying."

He cut her off with a slice of his hand. "Drop the act, Kiley. I'm neither deaf nor a fool. I understood every word your mother . . . ?" He lifted an eyebrow in the older woman's direction, prompting her to confirm his assumption.

"Lacey O'Dell," she offered coolly. She took a step in his direction, hand outstretched, but stopped dead in her tracks when Brutus bristled. She cautiously lowered her arm to her side, and Nicolò couldn't help noting with some satisfaction that it took her a few seconds to recover her aplomb. "Call me Lacey."

He continued to address Kiley, tearing at the tie knotted at his throat. "I understood every word Lacey said. You've been faking amnesia in order to pull off a scam meant to garner you a share of the Dante fire diamond mine."

"I did warn you," Lacey said to Kiley, before fixing him with an assessing gaze.

The pale blue color struck him as ice-cold and lacked the humor and kindness—not to mention the fiery passion—so often reflected in her daughter's. Maybe the difference between the two came from Lacey's additional years of running scams. Maybe this was how Kiley would appear a few years down such a rough and unforgiving road.

"I assume you're Nicolò Dante, Kiley's husband?" she asked.

"Is that what she told you?"

Lacey hesitated, disappointment flashing across her face. "Another lie?"

He stripped away his loosened tie and released the first few buttons of his shirt before it strangled him. "My lie, this time. Conning a con, I guess you'd call it."

Kiley caught her breath in a soft, disbelieving gasp. "No! No, that can't be. Tell me you didn't lie about that, Nicolò." She stared at him, her pleading look one of utter devastation. "Anything but that."

He met her gaze without saying a word. He simply waited. She knew the truth. She'd known from day one, minute one that they weren't married. And she'd chosen to play along every step of the way. No doubt her current performance was for her mother's benefit. Eventually she'd explain why she'd set this particular game in motion and what she hoped to gain from it. In the meantime, he was done playing.

At his continued silence, Kiley closed her eyes in abject surrender. The expression on her face absolutely gutted him, even though it had to be an act. It took her several seconds to regain her equilibrium and confront him again. When she did, her eyes were black with pain.

"We're not married? All those romantic dates you told me about, the seaside wedding, none of it ever happened?" When he didn't respond, she lifted a trembling hand to her mouth. "It's all a lie? *All of it?* Touring the city. Dantes Exclusive. Oh, God. Deseos. Those incredible, beautiful, romantic nights on Deseos. It was just a game to you?"

He didn't spare either of them. "It would seem we both lied, didn't we, Kiley?" But even that wasn't the complete truth. Because there had been times when he could have sworn there'd been nothing but honesty between them. "No doubt we each have our own special place reserved in hell."

"No! I don't believe you. Some of it had to be real."

Painfully aware of Lacey's keen interest, he cut Kiley off. He didn't want to remember any of it, remember what a fool he'd been. He especially refused to think about Deseos. "Enough. Just can the dramatics, will you? You've won your Oscar. I actually believed you had amnesia, if only for a few weeks."

Lacey blew out a sigh. "That's my daughter for you," she said with exaggerated sympathy. "Just one deception after another."

He turned on her next. "Like mother, like daughter?"

She stiffened, lifting her chin in defiance. "Not at all. Since you listened in on our conversation, you must have heard me say that I wanted no part in whatever scam Kiley's running."

"Very self-righteous of you," he said dryly. "I'd be a bit more impressed if I also hadn't heard you say you know better than to take on the Dantes. Still, I applaud your intelligence, as well as your keen sense of self-preservation."

She had the unmitigated gall to wink at him. "Thank you."

He removed his cufflinks and pocketed them before rolling up the sleeves of his shirt. Throughout the process, he continued to scrutinize her. "Just out of curiosity, what about the others?"

"What others?" Her movements slowed, stuttering to stillness, and she moistened her lips with the tip of her tongue. The "tell," the unconscious movement that warned him whenever she lied was painfully similar to the one he'd noticed Kiley use in the suite at Le Premier all those weeks ago. "I have no idea what you're talking about."

"I'm talking about the other men you've scammed over the years."

Lacey's eyes went flat and, if possible, even colder than before. "Hmm. I don't think I care for the direction this conversation has taken. So, if you don't mind, I think I'll opt out of it." She crossed to the sofa with a hip-swinging walk and gathered up her purse before confronting Kiley. "I believe you have something to give me."

The odd quality in her tone caused Brutus to leap to Kiley's defense. He muscled his way between the two women, appearing more ferocious and intimidating than Nicolò had ever seen him. With a muffled cry, Lacey stumbled back a few paces.

Kiley reached out and soothed the dog. "I have nothing for you. Do I, Brutus?"

He gave a sharp bark of agreement, one that had Lacey making a beeline for the doorway. Once she was satisfied, she stood a safe distance from the dog, she opened her mouth to argue. Sparing a swift glance toward Nicolò, she thought better of it. Apparently, he looked every bit as intimidating as his dog. It was a comforting thought.

"This isn't over," she warned. "Not by a long shot."

With that, she swept from the room escorted by Brutus, which no doubt explained why her heels tapped a frantic dance across the foyer. A few seconds later, the front door opened and slammed shut again. The silence hung in the air, thick and heavy. Nicolò could see Kiley struggling to find the right words to use on him. The best tack to explain away what he'd heard. He didn't give her the opportunity to settle on a strategy.

He approached, watching the wariness flare in her eyes. "When did you get your memory back? Or did you ever lose it in the first place?"

Her chin shot upward. "I lost it. I still don't remember anything before the accident, despite what you and my mother may think."

He couldn't help himself. He laughed, the sound harsh and ripe with disbelief. "Yeah, right."

She searched his face, no doubt looking for the chink in his armor, a chink he'd make very certain she never found. "There's nothing I can say to convince you I'm not faking amnesia, is there?"

"Not a thing."

Exhaustion settled over her, a visible blanket of weariness. "All right, fine, Nicolò. Have it your way. I'm lying about everything. I faked amnesia. Tell me what I've won. What's my consolation prize?"

He hesitated. "What are you talking about?"

"I must have faked amnesia for some reason." She spread her hands. "Tell me what I could possibly gain by such a pretense."

"Will half of Dantes' fire diamond mine do? I mean, when we first met at Le Premier that was your original scam, wasn't it?"

"For the sake of argument, let's say it was. Did it work?"

"You know it didn't."

"Why?"

His eyes narrowed in speculation. "What game are you playing now, Kiley?"

"Just answer the question. Why didn't it work?"

"Because your argument that day wasn't logical. You had all the documentation lined up, but it didn't make sense your family would have waited so many years before coming forward with the claim."

"Huh. Good point." It almost felt as though she were tiptoeing through her analysis, though he couldn't figure out why she bothered. "Okay, so I tried the con on you when we first met at Le Premier and it didn't work. Logically, what would I have done next?"

"Slipped away before I took legal action or involved the police."

"Then why didn't I? How would an amnesia scam work to my advantage? What do I gain by it?"

"You'd inveigle yourself into my life."

"Again, to what end? Money? I haven't asked and you haven't given me any. For the sex? Pretty damn good, I'll admit, but not worth the consequences when you found out about the scam. So, why would I assume such a risk? I had to know you'd take the precise steps you have and ask Juice to look into my background. If I were faking amnesia, that is."

He folded his arms across his chest. "You tell me. What could you possibly get out of pretending to lose your memory?"

"And there's the rub." For just an instant, humor lit her eyes before fading into something heartbreakingly bittersweet. "I haven't a clue. Maybe I fell in love with you when we first touched. Blame it on The Inferno, if that helps. Maybe I wanted a few days, a few precious weeks, to experience normalcy. No cons. No angle. Just a woman in love with a man with no strings attached."

He steeled himself not to reveal how her words had affected him. "And now?"

She lowered her head as though considering her options. Her hand slipped into her pocket, wrapping around something that crinkled. She froze, so still and silent, while conflict battled across her expression. And that's when it happened. She slowly looked up and he watched a hint of avarice grow in her eyes, watched them take on that hard, knowing look that had been so apparent in Lacey's gaze. She even managed to imitate her mother's flirtatious smile, the tip of her tongue tracing a tantalizing path along her lush mouth.

"I guess my little vacation from reality is over," she purred. "It's been fun. I got some designer clothes out of it, not to mention a trip to an island paradise. Of course, it didn't end as well as I'd hoped. But we'll just chalk that up to misfortune and move on."

"Kiley, what—"

"Don't," she said sharply, her breezy expression shattering for a telling moment. "It would never have worked, Nicolò. You must have known that as soon as you read my file. If we'd tried for anything more than a fling, my reputation would have ruined the Dante name. Just let me go. It's long past time I got back to my old life."

She was right and he knew it. "Fine. No point in dragging this out."

Without another word she headed for the foyer, picking up her purse from off the small hallway table where she'd left it. She hesitated with her hand on the front doorknob. "I appreciate you taking care of me after my accident."

Nicolò leaned against the archway between the living room and foyer. "Before you go, answer one question."

She shrugged without turning around. "Sure."

"Was any of it real?"

She swiveled to face him, but all he could see was Lacey staring at him through Kiley's eyes. "You mean, did I love you?"

"Did you?"

Her movements slowed, fluttering to stillness like a bird settling to its nest and she moistened her lips. "Sorry, Dante. I guess there was some sort of glitch in The Inferno that day at Le Premier. Our bond never took, at least not on my end of things. It may have been fun. But it wasn't true love." And with that, she walked out the door.

The instant it closed behind her, Brutus howled in anguish. "I'm right there with you, buddy," Nicolò whispered. "Right there with you."

Kiley never remembered the hours immediately following her flight from Nicolò's, where she went or what she did. She didn't awake to her surroundings until dusk had settled over the city and she found herself standing in front of a seedy little hotel somewhere in the Mission District.

A quick check of her wallet elicited five hundred dollars and a couple of credit cards. One was maxed out, so she used her precious cash, holding the second credit card in reserve. At least she now had a roof over her head. She huddled in the depressing little room she'd rented, her locket clutched in her hands, determined to come up with a game plan. The silver heart seemed to burn within her grasp, the lacey strips of silver pressing ridges into her palm, as though trying to imprint a message there.

But all she could think about was Nicolò. The expression on his face when he'd walked into the living room after overhearing her moth—No, *not* her mother—*Lacey*. That flash of emotion she'd seen in his eyes when he'd asked if any part of what they'd experienced over the past few weeks had been real. His shock when she'd shoved out the one lie she could ever remember telling.

She opened her hand and studied the locket, pushing absently at the intertwining strips of silver. She'd had to do it, had to lie to him. Once she'd absorbed that damning information from the file, she realized she couldn't stay. Couldn't allow her relationship with Nicolò to continue, assuming he'd have wanted such a thing. There'd been no other choice but to sever all remaining ties between them.

Even if Nicolò had been willing to overlook her past, she couldn't take the risk that one day her memory would come back and she'd transform into a younger version of Lacey. Couldn't risk the possibility she'd turn on him and use his wealth and position for her own personal gain. It didn't matter that walking away had broken her heart. After all she'd done to hurt others, it was a small price to pay.

And, regardless of what cost the sacrifice, she'd continue to pay until she put right all she'd set wrong in the past.

The instant she reached her decision one of the small strips of silver slid to one side and the locket clicked open. She stared in wonder at the small key she found nestled inside. If Lacey were right, it was the key to a safety deposit box, as well as the solution to her problem.

Because in that safety deposit box was the means for her to make amends to all those she'd injured over the years.

"Have you lost your mind?"

Nicolò glared at his brother, Lazz. "Why do you keep asking me that same question?"

"Because it bears repeating." He shoved a hand through his hair. "I mean, get serious. Did you not read her file?"

"Yes, I read her file."

"Did you not see the part that said scam artist in big red letters? Hell, it was hard to miss since Juice also put it in bolded caps."

"I saw it," Nicolò stated between gritted teeth.

"So then why the hesitation? She scammed every man she ever met, but she's not going to do the same to you because she's your Inferno soul mate?"

"That's part of it."

"And the other?"

"She's changed. She's not that person anymore."

Lazz's mouth dropped open and he floundered a moment before he could speak again. "You have got to be kidding me. You did not just say that."

Nicolò swore beneath his breath. He didn't know why it had taken him a full three hours after Kiley left before he caught the mistake within the lie. Maybe he'd been so focused on her claiming she didn't love him—and the "tell" which had given lie to that statement—that he hadn't fully processed her comment. But the instant it sank in, he realized she hadn't regained her memory at all, or she'd have known they never bonded at Le Premier.

As soon as he'd realized the truth, he'd gone charging out of the house. With Brutus at his side, he'd spent the entire night combing the city for her, but she'd disappeared as though she'd never existed. It was the first time in his entire life he hadn't been able to find a way out of a predicament. He was good at solving problems. The best. But this time he hit a brick wall and it was a wall he couldn't find a way over, under, or around, let alone through.

"She doesn't remember, Lazz," Nicolò insisted. "She still has amnesia."

"How can you possibly know?" Lazz argued.

"Because she slipped up right before she left. She said we first bonded at Le Premier. But we never did. We just spat sparks at each other. We weren't 'Infernoed' until I took her hand at the hospital."

"Hello. She's. A. Con. Artist. She hasn't changed. And it wasn't a slipup. It was an 'on purpose.' She was hoping you'd catch the mistake. Hoping you'd buy right back into the con. And damn it, Nicolò, you have, haven't you?"

"If that woman's still a con artist, then yeah, I'm buying it. And I'm going to keep buying it until I'm old and gray and we've been married for as many decades as Primo and Nonna." He leaned in, jaw set. "I'm going to find her, Lazz. And then I'm going to marry her. She's going to have my sons—and I say sons because, with the exception of our cousin, Gianna, the men in our family seem incapable of producing daughters. We're going to have four of them, in case you're interested. And anyone who has a problem with that can discuss it first with my right fist and then with my left hook."

He looked around with a hint of defiance, stunned when he caught Sev and Marco's nod of approval. Even better was the expression Primo wore, one that offered unconditional support. "Everyone should receive a second chance," his grandfather stated.

Nicolò turned on Lazz again, his determination rock-solid. "So, are you going to help me find her, or are you going to fight me over this?"

"You know I don't believe in the family curse," Lazz muttered.

"Blessing," the others chorused in unison.

Nicolò barked out a laugh, the first one since Kiley left him. "You better start believing in The Inferno, Lazz. So far, it's three down. You're the only one of us left."

"And that's the way it's going to stay." Lazz held up his hands before anyone could argue the point. "Fine. You want her, you got her."

Nicolò nodded. "Let's just hope it's that easy."

Chapter Ten

Of course, it wasn't easy at all. It took a team effort involving Juice and the entire Dante family to finally locate Kiley. Nicolò couldn't recall a rougher few weeks. Not that he had anyone to blame other than himself. He'd allowed her to walk out instead of stopping her, and that knowledge had haunted him every single minute since. When the call finally came in from Juice, he found it a struggle just to form a coherent sentence.

"Where is she?" he managed to ask.

"A small dive down in the Mission District bearing the delightful name of the Riff Raff Inn. Not one I'd recommend, especially not for a woman on her own."

Nicolò swore. "What the hell is she doing there?"

"I can't say. Might be all she could afford. Thank God she finally used plastic or we'd have had the devil's own time finding her."

Nicolò closed his eyes. Of course. She'd left with nothing in hand but the funds in her purse.

Five hundred couldn't have kept her fed and housed for much longer than a couple weeks, if that. Not in San Francisco. What would she have done if she hadn't had another source of money? Would she have come back to him? Somehow he doubted it.

"Watch the motel in case she leaves," Nicolò instructed. "I'll be there in fifteen."

"You'd better make it ten."

Hell. "Why? What's wrong?"

"Our old buddy Ferrell just got out of a cab. He's making tracks toward the motel and looks like a man on a mission. Do you want me to intercept him?"

"Not unless there's trouble. It can't be a coincidence he's shown up, or much doubt who he's there to see. Follow him and call me back with a room number. I'm leaving now."

He was five minutes out when Juice called again. "More good news," came the head of security's gloomy voice. "By the look of things, Kiley's about to have another visitor."

"Who?"

"Based on the description you gave me, I'm guessing it's Lacey O'Dell. Blonde, blue eyes, five foot nothing. Looks a good bit like Kiley, except . . ."

"Harder," Nicolò supplied.

"I'd call her cold if she didn't look spitting mad. If I were a betting man, I'd say your wife, er, sorry—Ms. O'Dell has done something to seriously tick off Momma dearest."

"Which room is Kiley in?"

"Two-oh-nine. Up the stairs, hang a right. Middle of the hallway on the left. You'll find me near the stairwell. I can see the door, but I'm not close enough to hear anything. Don't want to attract too much attention from those inside."

"Will I have any trouble getting past the front desk?"

"I wasn't sure what sort of reception you might receive when you joined the party, so I dropped a Franklin on the manager. He's suddenly developed a severe case of deaf, dumb, and blind."

"Hang tight. I'm almost there."

A few minutes later, Nicolò swung into a parking space and hustled into the motel. Juice's bribe worked. The manager didn't so much as lift his head, just gestured toward a worn stairway carpeted in the remains of faded paisley. Nicolò came across Juice in the hallway, a few doors up from Kiley's room.

"In there," he muttered, pointing. "Decided I better move closer so I could step in if things turned nasty. Got a right little row going."

More than a row. Nicolò could hear Ferrell's voice raised in fury, as well as Lacey's. And then he heard Kiley's cry of alarm and didn't bother with a civilized knock on the door. He crashed against the hollow core panel and sent the door bursting inward.

It took only an instant to assess the situation. Ferrell and Lacey were in a furious struggle over something that glittered with unmistakable fire. A diamond necklace. Or rather, what remained of a diamond necklace. And then he saw Kiley. She was on the floor, a hand raised to her cheek, one that showed evidence of a rapidly growing bruise. He was at her side in an instant, lifting her in his arms and clear of the fray. He didn't know who had hit her or why, but someone would pay for hurting her.

"Are you okay?"

"I'm fine." She ran her hands across his chest while she ate him up with her eyes. "Don't think me ungrateful, but . . . What are you doing here?"

He pulled a slow smile. "I'm here to rescue you, of course. Isn't that how it's supposed to work?"

She shook her head, despite the hope dawning in her expression. "Only in fairy tales. Not in real life."

"In real life, too, sweetheart. Now, who hit you?"

"It was an accident."

"Uh-huh." He shot Lacey and Ferrell a grim look. "Don't go anywhere. I'll be right back."

"Forget it, Nicolò. This is my fight, too."

Together they waded into the fray, separating the two combatants. Lacey gave a squeak of surprise and broke away from Ferrell with only minor prompting from Kiley. The older man backed up several paces, the remains of a diamond necklace clutched in his hand.

"If you don't want to find yourself eating carpet with a bruise to match Kiley's, I suggest you hand over that necklace."

"I'm not handing over anything," Ferrell snarled. "The diamonds are mine."

"I paid you what you were owed," Nicolò bit out. "And a good deal more beside. Or have you forgotten that minor detail?"

Kiley balled her hands into fists. "Why, you lying piece of scum. You told me you didn't receive so much as a dime from the Dantes."

"Look who's calling who scum," he shot back. "I deserve the diamonds for the hell you put me through. You deserve to know what it feels like to get conned."

"I'm not going to warn you again," Nicolò interrupted. "Drop the necklace."

Ferrell glared in frustration. "You don't understand."

"No, you don't understand." Nicolò stalked closer, leaned in so the other man couldn't mistake his words. "I'm going to pretend that bruise on Kiley's cheek is a regrettable accident. That it didn't have anything to do with you. While I'm operating under that misapprehension, I suggest you get as far from this room as physically possible. You got me?"

Ferrell's hand clenched around the necklace, common sense in a pitched battle with greed. After an endless minute, sensibility won out, though it took on a vindictive edge. "Fine. I'll leave. But you're a fool, Dante. She's just going to use you the same way she's used every other man she's ever met." He shook his head in disgust. "You're going to wish you'd never met her before she's finished with you."

And with that, he threw down the remains of the necklace and stalked from the room. He attempted to slam the door behind him, but it listed drunkenly on its hinges and wouldn't close.

"Thank you for getting rid of him," Lacey said, offering Nicolò a beaming smile. "You can come to my rescue any time."

"My pleasure, though I'm here to rescue Kiley, not you."

He couldn't help but notice that Lacey's smile was absolutely symmetrical, no adorable tilt to disturb its perfection. She bent down and scooped up the necklace, allowing a brief frown to carve a network of lines between her brows and at the corners of her mouth.

"Damn," she muttered. "What the hell were you thinking, Kiley?"

Kiley shrugged. "You know what I was thinking. And FYI, my plans haven't changed just because of a bruised cheek."

"What happened to the necklace?" he asked. "Where are the rest of the diamonds?"

Lacey jumped in before Kiley could respond. "She grew a conscience, that's what." She shot a sour look at Nicolò. "Your bad influence, no doubt."

"I gather the necklace originally belonged to Cameron O'Dell?" At Lacey's nod, he held out his hand. "Do you mind?"

"Not much left of it." A wistful expression slipped through her gaze. "You should have seen it before Kiley broke it up. It was spectacular."

He scrutinized the remaining diamonds. There were three of them, two single carat diamonds as well as a gorgeous five-carat stone that had to be one of the most exquisite fire diamonds he'd ever seen. "Magnificent."

"It was."

Unable to last another second without touching some part of Kiley, he drew her to the bed, and urged her down on the edge. Then he lifted her chin and tilted her face into the light. "That's quite a shiner you have there. I was right, wasn't I? Ferrell did this?"

"He didn't hit me on purpose," she conceded. "He and Lacey were fighting to get their hands on the necklace and my cheekbone got in the way of his elbow."

"Ouch." He glanced at Lacey and jerked his head toward the door. "Why don't you get your daughter some ice."

"Oh, of course. Right away." Not a trace of sarcasm rippled through her words, yet she managed to make her displeasure heard loud and clear. Quite a feat. "Only too happy to help."

As soon as she left the room, he asked, "What's going on, Kiley? How did you end up with the necklace?"

She shrugged. "I figured out how to open the locket."

He lifted an eyebrow. "And the necklace was inside?"

That won him a brief, endearingly lopsided smile. "No, but the key to a safety deposit box was. It took me a while to track down the right bank. But once I had, I found the necklace."

His eyes narrowed at that telling piece of information. Did she even realize what she'd said? By admitting she didn't know how to open the locket or where she'd stashed the necklace, she'd just confirmed she still had amnesia. He let it pass for now. "And after you found the necklace? What did you do then?"

"I used the list, the list from the file I found on your desk."

"What did you use it for?" he asked gently.

She focused on a spot over his shoulder, her face set in determined lines. "I gave the diamonds to the people I—" Her voice broke for an instant before she regained control over it. "To the people I scammed. Ferrell was the last one. I didn't realize you'd already paid him off or I'd never have contacted him."

"I gather he wasn't satisfied with a single diamond?"

"Even the little one was worth twice what I took from him. But he felt he deserved more for his pain and suffering. He wanted all three. Then Lacey arrived and . . ." She shrugged.

"Then I jumped into the fray. Got it."

Her gaze drifted to his face again. Clung. "How did you find me?"

The Inferno called to him, urging him to lean in and take her mouth, to drink her in like a man lost and parched and desperate for relief. He fought the sensation. Not yet. Not until they'd resolved all the remaining issues. "I've been searching for you almost from the moment you left."

"Almost," she repeated.

"Well, I had to come to my senses first," he admitted. "When I couldn't find you, I elicited some help from my family."

"Your family?" She shook her head in disbelief. "They were willing to help you find me?"

"Every last one of them," he confirmed.

She stared in wonder. "But why would they do that? Didn't they know what was in the file?"

"They knew."

"I don't understand any of this."

Before she could ask any more questions, Lacey returned with a bucket of ice. Playing the role of the concerned parent, she filled a washcloth with the cubes and offered it to Kiley. "There you go, sweetheart. This should help."

"Now it's your turn," Nicolò warned.

Lacey released a gusty sigh. "I had a feeling I wasn't going to get out of this unscathed."

"I'm surprised you came back. I half expected you to take off."

"Thought about it," she admitted.

"Why didn't you?"

She gave him a cheeky grin. "You have the diamonds."

Of course. Foolish to think she wouldn't make a final play for them. "Explain the necklace. And Kiley's scam with the fire diamond mine."

She lifted an eyebrow, a calculating expression sliding into her gaze. "What do I get in return?"

"Lacey!" Kiley protested.

"The two little ones," Nicolò offered.

"No way. I want the big one."

"That belongs to Kiley," he said in a voice that didn't brook any argument. "If you want the little ones, you're going to need to explain since Kiley can't."

Lacey made a face. "She really doesn't remember, does she? If she did, she'd never have given away the diamonds."

"I am still here, you know," Kiley objected.

Lacey patted her shoulder. "Of course you are, dear. I assume you showed Nicolò all of Cameron O'Dell's documentation? Birth certificate, death certificate, will?"

Nicolò waited while Kiley silently fumed, fully aware that she had no idea how to answer her mother's question. Satisfied Lacey's point had been made, he answered in Kiley's place, "Yes, I saw all that. What happened to Cameron's share of the mine?"

"He sold it to his brother before your grandfather, Primo, made his offer. He sold it in exchange—"

"For the necklace."

"Exactly. He thought the mine was played out. As did his brother, Seamus, for that matter."

"Got it. And you and Kiley have been using the necklace to run a series of scams. Selling and reselling it, I assume, then either substituting a fake or cutting out before the transaction was completed?"

She hesitated. "Well, not exactly." She shot a disgruntled look toward her daughter. "I guess since there's no more necklace, I can tell you the truth."

Kiley braced herself. "I'm not sure I can handle much more truth right now."

"Most of those things in the file?" Lacey shrugged. "It was me. I'm the one responsible."

"No." Kiley shook her head, adamant. "That's not possible. Those people identified me by name. Ferrell even knew about my birthmark.

"Yes, well." Lacey lowered her gaze and released a light laugh. "The others might have identified you because I used your name and colored my hair to match. Ferrell knew about the birthmark because I have a matching one. Though, I suspect he knew damn well you weren't me. He probably figured out the connection and went with it, hoping the Dantes wouldn't figure out it was me, not you."

"You—" Kiley took a deep breath and tried again. "You would do that to your own daughter? Why?"

Lacey waved the question aside with a sweep of her well-manicured hand. "A girl's got to survive. And speaking of surviving . . ." She spun to face Nicolò. "Cough it up, handsome. I explained everything, now I want my diamonds."

"What about my scamming the Dantes?" Kiley pressed.

She spared her daughter a quick look. "Sorry, sweetie. That one's on you. I had no part in it." She spared Nicolò a quick look and made a gimme motion with her fingers.

He removed the largest of the stones from the band and pocketed it before handing her the remaining two. "I'll be watching to make sure that you don't use Kiley's name anytime in the future," he warned.

"Not a problem. And now, if you'll excuse me, I do believe I've outstayed my welcome. If there's one thing I've learned, it's how to make a graceful exit." She flashed a megawatt smile at them both. "Don't worry, I won't be in touch."

"I'll see you out," Nicolò insisted.

They didn't speak until they'd reached the foyer. He pulled a business card from his pocket and handed it to her. "I hope you won't need this, but just in case."

She regarded it in surprise. "I don't understand. Why are you giving this to me?"

"Two reasons. When all is said and done, you're still Kiley's mother. Family means a lot to the Dantes."

She shrugged that off as though it didn't count for much. Which, he supposed, it didn't. Not for her. "And the other?" she asked.

"The other is for the lie you just told in there. Although I wouldn't advise lying to me anytime in the future. I'll always know."

"That's so sweet." She twinkled up at him. "You're actually thanking me."

Before he could debate the point, his soon-to-be mother-in-law swept out the door and disappeared down the street with a jaunty hip-swinging stride. And wasn't the idea of a familial connection with Lacey a depressing thought? He didn't waste any further time on her. After giving Juice the money to pay for the damaged door, he sent the Dantes' head of security on his way. Then Nicolò returned to the room where he'd left his heart and soul.

Kiley stood by the motel window, staring in the direction her mother had taken. He joined her there, taking her hand in his. "I'm sorry, sweetheart. I'm sorry for doubting you. I'm sorry for allowing you to leave. And I'm even more sorry I didn't find you sooner."

"What do you want, Nicolò? I mean, really." She lifted her gaze to his and he flinched at the wealth of sorrow he found there. "As much as I appreciate your helping me out of a tight spot, what is there left to be said?"

"Just one more thing." He cupped her face. "I love you, Kiley O'Dell. I love you more than I believed it possible to love someone. I want to spend the rest of my life with you and I'm hoping that's what you want, too."

"I love you, Nicolò. I do." Her voice broke. "I always have."

"Marry me. For real this time. No more lies. No more deception. From this day on, cards on the table."

She shook her head, pain etched deep in her face. "Even now you're not leveling with me. After all we've been through, you still haven't put all your cards on the table."

"What are you—"

"Stop it, Nicolò. I know she lied. I'm not the victim she made me out to be."

He sucked in a deep breath. "How did you know?"

"I'm not a fool. I read the files. Every last word. Those men weren't describing my mother. They were describing me. When I met with them, when I made reparations, they recognized me. They—" She fought to gather her self-control. "They despised me. Me, not her."

"She's no innocent in all this."

"No, she's not. I suppose she tried to make amends by taking the blame for all those scams." Her mouth trembled, ripping him to shreds. "But I can't marry you. Not ever. It wouldn't be right."

He fought the panic turning his insides to ice water. "Don't do this, Kiley. The past doesn't matter."

"You're wrong. If it didn't matter, I wouldn't have given away those diamonds. Trust me. It matters. It matters even more when you have nothing left but your honor and self-respect."

"You're not the person you once were."

"I am that person," she insisted. "I'll always have to live with that knowledge. So will you, and so will your family. So will your friends and associates and customers. And they may not be as forgiving as you when they find out who—*what*—I am."

"Was, Kiley. *Was.* Don't you get it? I don't care. I love you. We belong together."

"Do you think I don't want to spend the rest of my life in your arms? Oh, Nicolò. I love you so much. But I can't be with you. I can't marry you."

"*Why?*"

The words burst out. "Because one day I'll wake up and I'll remember. And when that happens, I'll turn back into her. I won't have a choice. She's who I really am. Who I'm meant to be. I can't do that to you. I won't."

"Bullshit!" He broke off, drawing in a deep, calming breath. "Do you really believe you have no choice? That you can't change? Do you want to be the woman you were before?"

"No. *No.*"

"Then don't. It's that simple. When you remember—*if* you remember—you can choose. You can choose a life filled with love and family. Or you can choose to go back to your old lifestyle. I'm betting you'll like your new life far better than your old one."

"It's not that easy," she protested. "It can't be."

"It can and it is." He pulled her close, closing his eyes in relief when he felt the helpless give of her body. It told him he hadn't lost her, that he only had to find the right words to win her. Honest words. Words from the heart. "If someday you remember, if it becomes a struggle, I'll be there for you. I swear it. And so will my family. There's only one thing that matters, Kiley. Do you love me?"

"You know I do." Her breath shuddered from her lungs. "I don't want to be her, Nicolò. I don't *ever* want to be her."

He understood she didn't just mean her past self, but the sort of woman her mother had become, as well. "You're not. Who you are now, without the baggage from the past, is the true woman. Your innate sweetness and strength, your intelligence and humor, your wit. All of that existed at the core of you. That's the real you. That's the woman I fell in love with, the Kiley you would have been if your life had taken a different turn." His arms tightened around her and he put every ounce of grit and determination into his voice. "Well, it did make that turn, sweetheart. Call it fate. Or divine intervention. Hell, call it The Inferno. But because of your accident, you have a chance to take your life in a new direction. With me."

He cupped her face and kissed his way past the tears, losing himself in her passionate warmth. This was the Kiley he knew. The Kiley he'd fallen in love with. The Inferno caught fire, blazing hotter than he'd ever felt it before. It was almost as though by their breaking through the final barriers separating them, by sharing those final pieces of themselves, The Inferno rewarded them with a connection so strong, so utterly complete, that nothing could ever divide them again.

He lifted his head and gazed down at her with unfettered honesty and trust. "Marry me, Kiley. Take a chance. Create a brand-new life with me."

"Cards on the table from now on?"

"All fifty-two of them."

She smiled then, that beautiful, radiant, lopsided smile. "Take me home, Nicolò."

He didn't need any further prompting. Together they left behind the old and forgotten, the sordid and painful, and walked into a future shiny with possibility.

Epilogue

Kiley's memory did return, but not for another twenty years.

It came back on a hot summer day while she played baseball with her husband, her four strapping sons, and their various first and second cousins. Nicolò had suggested she play centerfield, "out of harm's way," but she'd insisted on covering third. What she hadn't anticipated was chasing an easy pop fly that took an unexpected curve into a nearby street.

It happened again as it had twice before in her life. She darted out into the street, her glove lifted skyward, only afterward realizing the sheer idiocy of her reckless actions. The driver of the oncoming car hit his brakes and horn at the exact same moment, skidding toward her at a frightening speed. She knew she wouldn't be able to avoid the impact this time, just as she hadn't on that very first occasion when she'd been struck by a cab outside of Le Premier. Ironically, this car was the same bright yellow as the cab had been all those years ago. This time it wouldn't miss her, just as it hadn't then. And this time she'd fully suffer the consequences of her impulsiveness.

At the last possible instant, an arm swooped around her waist like a band of iron and yanked her clear of the oncoming car. With a final blare of the horn, it swept past, leaving her trembling within Nicolò's embrace. Her husband growled out a string of Italian curses before kissing her senseless.

When she surfaced from the kiss, it was to find her sons grouped around her in a tight worried circle, and her husband gazing down at her with a combination of undisguised love and bone-deep terror. It felt as though time caught its breath for a brief instant, pausing just long enough for the rush of memories to finish cycling through her head, cascading over her in a dizzying flood.

In that odd timeless moment, she remembered it all. Those crazed early years with her mother. The childhood better off forgotten. The lessons she'd learned at the knee of an amoral parent more concerned with material possessions than character or soul. More concerned with money than the needs of a lonely child desperate for a proper mother. Kiley could see, as though through a thick glass, the string of scams she and her mother had pulled. Could feel the cold emptiness of that life, could feel the spirit draining out of her with each successive con.

"Mom?" Dominic, her eldest, touched her shoulder, fear evident in the deep black gaze he kept trained on her face. "You okay?

"I—"

The past tugged at her. Called to her. Tried to pull her back toward that other person. That person she'd been all those years ago. So many options opened themselves to her, options that for that long-ago Kiley would have been like hitting a multi-million dollar jackpot.

And then she began to laugh. She'd hit the jackpot long ago. She gazed up at her husband, a man she adored with all her heart and soul, a man who'd saved her from that other life. And she looked at each one of the children she'd given birth to, children she'd showered with love and attention, discipline and a strong moral character. And she laughed again, laughed for sheer joy. The diamond on her wedding ring flamed brighter than ever. It was the last diamond from Cameron O'Dell's fire diamond necklace, a diamond that symbolized an end to the old and the opportunity for a new beginning.

Go back?

Never.

She picked up the softball laying at her feet and tagged her son with it. "You're out," she told him. "Now, let's play ball."

The Dante Inferno continues with Lazz's story!

Lazz's Contract Marriage by Day Leclaire

Meet Day Leclaire

I love family first and foremost, which is why writing a family saga is so much fun. Maybe you can tell that from my books since they always feature the warmth and joy that comes from having a close-knit family. I also love animals and have taken in rescue dogs and cats and fostered dogs for the local animal shelter. And of course, I love writing. All I need is a functioning brain (batteries not included), a pen, and paper, and I can write anywhere. Please don't let a conversation with me lag because my imagination takes over and I. Am. Checked. Out!

USA Today bestselling author, Day Leclaire is the author of more than 60 novels and has received an impressive eleven nominations for the romance industry's most prestigious award, Romance Writers of America RITA© Award. Day lives in Charlotte, NC and spends her days obsessively writing while vaguely remembering to pay attention to her adorable husband, busy son and daughter-in-law, two tiny grandchildren, and two even tinier Teddy Bear dogs. Not to mention a whole lot of dust!

Thank you so much for taking the time to read **The Dante Inferno:** *The Dante Dynasty Series*. I hope you enjoy this very special Italian-American family. I love hearing from my readers. For a personal response, please contact me at Day@DayLeclaire.com. And be sure to visit my website at www.DayLeclaire.com. Sign up for my newsletter for my latest releases and insider info available nowhere else! Just visit: https://www.dayleclaire.com/join-my-mailing-list

You can also find me on Facebook at www.facebook.com/Day.Leclaire.Private and Twitter at www.Twitter.com/DayLeclaire.